Kate told Rhyno how much she disliked him

She should have anticipated his response, but she didn't, and the next instant she found herself locked in a fierce embrace. She was too stunned at first to react, but when she finally struggled against those imprisoning arms, her efforts merely made her more aware of the male hardness of his body. Then every nerve and pulse began to throb with a strange rhythm that sent an incredible weakness surging into her limbs.

She should have felt insulted, but instead she found herself responding, until she felt drugged and no longer capable of coherent thought.

Rhyno released her abruptly, and she staggered away from him. She felt dazed, and she had a horrible feeling it showed on her face, while his remained composed and shuttered.

D0090163

YVONNE WHITTAL

late harvest

Harlequin Books

TORONTO • NEW YORK • LOS ANGELES • LONDON
AMSTERDAM • PARIS • SYDNEY • HAMBURG
STOCKHOLM • ATHENS • TOKYO • MILAN

For those fantastic
wine farmers of the Cape
who, through their magical skills,
have produced the superb wines
South Africa is noted for,
and which my family and I
enjoy so much.

———————————————◆———————————————

Harlequin Presents first edition February 1983
ISBN 0-373-10574-6

Original hardcover edition published in 1982
by Mills & Boon Limited

CHAPTER ONE

THE vines hung heavy with grapes in the merciless sun, the green berries swollen with the nectar of the gods. They were ready to harvest, but the old slave bell had not rung that morning to herald the start of that joyous, fruitful season. It had stood silent and motionless beneath the shade of the old oaks, and the workers, instead of filling the vineyards with their usual laughter and gaiety, were sombre-faced and dressed in their Sunday best as they filed along the path towards Solitaire's small cemetery.

Kate Duval stood between her aunt, Edwina Duval, and Hubert Walton the attorney. Tall, slim, and with silvery fair hair that fell straight down to her shoulders, Kate's paleness was accentuated by the severe black dress which was devoid of trimmings, and she wore no other adornment apart from the pearl pendant which hung about her neck like a single tear. Sapphire blue eyes, lacking in their usual fire, stared fixedly at the coffin being slowly lowered into the newly dug grave. 'Ashes to ashes; dust to dust,' the parson's voice droned on to a halt, and pearly white teeth bit into a quivering lip to steady it. The breeze sighed through the tall cypress trees, and rose petals fluttered from Kate's fingers as a final tribute to find a resting place on the polished wooden box containing her father's body.

Rock of ages, cleft for me,
Let me hide myself in thee.

The clear, melodious voices of the estate workers sang the age-old hymn through to its conclusion, the last notes fading to become one with the gentle breeze stirring the leaves in the trees.

7

It was a silent procession of mourners that made their way back to Solitaire's homestead. After the elaborate funeral service in Stellenbosch, the burial out at Solitaire was a private affair with only the closest family present, but the latter was not strictly true. Hubert Walton, a tall, wiry man in his late fifties, attended the burial in his capacity as family friend and attorney, and the estate manager, Rhyno van der Bijl, was accompanied by his mother, a tall, well-proportioned woman who was greying attractively across the temples.

Kate, with her arm linked through Aunt Edwina's, led the procession into the gabled house with its spacious, airy rooms where Jacques Duval's distinctive presence still lingered prominently, although his gravelly voice was forever silent.

Lunch was served in the large dining hall, and Solitaire Estate wine was poured from crystal decanters into delicate stemmed glasses. The servants came and went silently from the room where the conversation was subdued. The atmosphere was tense, but there was also an undeniable hint of expectancy attached to it. Jacques Duval had been known for his wealth and generosity, and it was perhaps for this reason that everyone awaited the reading of his will with such mixed emotions; everyone, that was, except Kate, who was more concerned at that moment with her efforts to keep her tears at bay.

Solitaire was a flourishing wine-producing estate, and the imposing, historical house dated back to 1694. The original owner was reputed to have been a close friend of one of the leaders of the revolt against the governor of the Cape during that impossible period when the wine farmers suffered crippling losses as a result of bribery and corruption. A rapid succession of owners had followed until Pierre Duval had bought Solitaire a century ago, but it was his grandson, Jacques Duval, who had over the past thirty-one years turned Solitaire into one of the most profitable wine estates in the Stellenbosch area.

The conversation at the lunch table was beginning to curdle like over-heated custard, but Aunt Edwina's timing was perfect. An almost unnoticeable signal brought the house servants into the dining hall, and when they stood respectfully along the nearest wall Hubert Walton lifted his attaché case on to the table. There was a sudden hush, and everyone's eyes had became riveted to the important legal document which the attorney took out of his case, but Kate's glance somehow roamed the length of the table.

Her father's younger brother, François, was there with his wife, Dixie, and their two sons, Peter and Cedric. The only time Kate could recall them paying a visit to Solitaire was when their financial status had dipped so low that her father had had to write out a substantial cheque to set them back on their feet, and that had occurred three times during the twenty-two years since Kate's birth. Farther down the table sat Wendy and Richard Brandt, the children of her father's youngest sister, Nancy, who had died some years ago. Their father had been an alcoholic who had battered his wife and children almost as regularly as one would wind a clock. What followed became an accepted ritual. Nancy would arrive on Solitaire with her children, and Jacques would support them until Ivan Brandt had managed to pull himself out of his alcoholic stupor again to take care of his family. Kate had been fond of her cousins, Wendy and Richard, but they had grown from bewildered, insecure children into unpleasant, demanding adults. They had both been in their late teens when their father had died under the wheels of a truck while in an inebriated condition, and their mother had died not many years later. Since then they had come to Solitaire often, demanding and usually getting the financial aid they were seeking.

Kate turned her head slightly and her glance collided with Rhyno van der Bijl's. His dark eyes held hers boldly, almost challengingly, and the resentment which she had carried around within her these past eighteen months flared to the surface. She disliked this tall, lean man with his dark hair cropped close to his well-shaped head, and the aristocratic features which could have been chiselled out of bronze. As always his expression was stern and severe, and she had seldom seen him smile except in the company of her father. He always dressed well, but his choice of clothes was sober, and it left one with the impression that he was much older than his thirty years. With a degree in viticulture, and several years' experience in all the facets of wine farming, he was an asset to Solitaire, but Kate resented his presence for the simple reason that he was in the position for which she had prepared herself so rigorously since childhood.

Naomi van der Bijl sat next to her son, and she looked ill at ease as if she considered herself an intruder. Kate had met her only once before, and then it had been very briefly, but she knew this woman's history a great deal better. Naomi had inherited La Reine, the farm lying adjacent to Solitaire. La Reine had been in the du Pré family for more years than Solitaire had been owned by the Duvals, but Naomi had made the mistake of marrying William van der Bijl, and he had remained with her only long enough to squander the du Pré fortune. Left destitute with a small son to take care of, Naomi had tried to raise La Reine to its former glory, but her husband's mismanagement had had far-reaching reffects, and lack of funds had finally forced her to sell the farm she had loved so much. Jacques Duval had bought it, and La Reine had been incorporated into the Solitaire Estate twenty years ago. La Reine now took almost every available prize at the wine shows for its superb quality red wines, while Solitaire was noted for its white wines.

It had taken barely a few seconds for these thoughts to flash through Kate's mind before Hubert Walton cleared his throat, and the reading of her father's will began.

The legal language used in such documents made little sense to Kate at first, but gradually, as she observed the dark, angry clouds building up in the faces of her family, she began to realise what was happening. Jacques Duval had excluded his brother François from his will, and neither had he left anything to Nancy's children.

'They had received more than their fair share from Solitaire funds during my lifetime,' her father had stated in his will.

Pandemonium broke loose! Chairs toppled as irate members of the family leapt to their feet, nasty accusations were flung at the attorney and at Kate, and doors were slammed as they stormed out of the house, vowing never to set foot on Solitaire again.

Hubert Walton smiled wryly. '*That*, I think, is what your father hoped to achieve,' he informed Kate, whose delicate features had gone a shade paler. 'He didn't want you saddled with them during *your* lifetime as well.'

Kate could not have answered him even if she had wanted to, her throat felt too tight, but his remark fortunately did not require a reply, and the reading of the will continued.

Jacques Duval had left a considerable sum of money to each of his trustworthy servants, and Kate swallowed convulsively when the sound of muffled sobs reached her ears. They shuffled out of the room moments later, leaving only Rhyno, Naomi, Kate, and Aunt Edwina to hear the remainder of Jacques Duval's will.

'To my dear sister Edwina,' Hubert's voice went on, 'I leave a yearly allowance of fifteen thousand rand, and express the wish that she will make Solitaire her home for as long as she lives.' While Aunt Edwina fumbled for her lace handkerchief, Hubert's glance travelled towards Rhyno's mother. 'Lastly, I bequeath the sum of thirty thousand rand to Naomi van der Bijl (née du Pré). She has always had my admiration and respect.'

'But I can't accept it!' Naomi van der Bijl protested with a mixture of astonishment and indignation. 'I've never done anything to deserve it, and it wouldn't be right!'

'It was Jacques' wish that you receive this legacy, and he was most adamant about it,' Hubert Walton assured her, and Naomi glanced helplessly from Edwina to her son before a peculiar look of forced resignation flitted across her face.

'I presume there's more to this will,' Rhyno broke the strained silence, and Hubert Walton frowned heavily.

'There is,' he said, glancing apologetically at Naomi who was seated a little distance from Kate. 'The rest of this will concerns only Miss Edwina Duval, your son, and Kate.'

Naomi and Rhyno exchanged curious glances, then she nodded and rose to her feet. 'I'll wait in the living-room.'

A peculiar tension spiralled through Kate when the door closed behind Rhyno's mother, and her hands tightened involuntarily in her lap. She had a distinct feeling that she was not going to like what she was about to hear, and when the attorney avoided her direct gaze she was alerted to something she was as yet unaware of.

Hubert cleared his throat once more, and the hands that held the legal document shook slightly, but his voice was steady when he read out Jacques Duval's final wishes.

'The Estate, as it stands, and with all further assets, liquid or otherwise, shall be dealt with as follows: My daughter, Katharine Duval, and my estate manager, Rhyno van der Bijl, shall jointly inherit the entire estate on condition that they are married within thirty days of my death. If, after a year, their marriage is not a success, then Rhyno van der Bijl shall take possession of his rightful heritage, La Reine, and my daughter Katharine shall inherit Solitaire.'

'Just a minute!' Rhyno interrupted when Hubert paused for breath, and his deep, harsh voice scraped along Kate's raw nerves where she sat staring white-faced at the attorney. 'You surely don't expect us to either believe or accept what you've just read there?'

'It's here in black and white, Rhyno.'

'It's preposterous!' Kate choked out the words as she emerged from her stunned state, and she almost followed the example of her departed relatives by knocking over her chair as she leapt to her feet. 'I refuse to—to marry this man in order to inherit what's rightfully mine!'

Hubert lowered his eyes to the papers before him, and said decisively, 'If you want Solitaire, Kate, then you'll have no option.'

'What exactly does that mean?' Rhyno demanded, the skin stretching tautly across his lean, hard face.

'It means, Rhyno, that if you and Kate refuse to marry each other, then Solitaire goes to Edwina. After her death it will be sold, and the money will be distributed amongst several charities which I have listed here.'

'And La Reine?' Rhyno bit out the words.

'La Reine will be sold at once, and several charitable organisations will benefit from its sale.'

Rhyno paled visibly beneath his tanned complexion, and his sensual mouth thinned with a touch of ruthlessness. A tiny nerve pulsed against his temple, and when his eyes met Kate's it felt to her as if those dark eyes were boring right into her with something close to hatred.

Shaken, she lowered herself into her chair once more and turned to the woman seated beside her. 'Did you know about this, Aunt Edwina?'

A scented lace handkerchief fluttered, and Edwina looked away uncomfortably. 'I knew about it, but——'

'I told Edwina this morning so that it wouldn't be such a shock to her now,' Hubert Walton intervened calmly, and Kate felt like screaming. How dared he take this whole thing so calmly when her entire world had suddenly been turned upside down!

'I'll *buy* Solitaire, if that's the only way I can get it without plunging myself into a marriage I don't want,' she almost hissed out the words.

'How will you buy it, Kate?' Hubert asked, an expression closely resembling pity flitting across his lined face. 'With a five thousand rand a year legacy I can't see you doing that, can you?'

Kate stared at him in stunned silence, her eyes wide, and the pupils dilated, then she asked incredulously, 'Is that all I'll get?'

'If you don't carry out your father's wishes, yes,' Hubert nodded solemnly.

'Oh, my God!' she cried hoarsely, burying her white face in her trembling hands, and wondering just how much more of this she could take.

A chair scraped on the polished wooden floor, the sound jarring her nerves, then Rhyno's voice broke the strained silence. 'Is there anything else we ought to know?'

Hubert shook his grey head. 'Not at the moment, no.'

'In that case I hope you'll excuse me,' Rhyno said abruptly, and without a second glance in their direction he strode out of the dining hall and closed the door quietly but decisively behind him.

Kate watched him go with a coldness spreading through her insides, then her lifeless glance travelled down the length of the table towards the chair her father had always occupied. He would never sit there at the head of the long table again, but even in death he ruled her future as he had ruled over the estate during his lifetime. Her father had not been a harsh man, and he had showered her with love and affection since her mother's death so many years ago, but he had always been extremely firm with her. There had been times when he had been totally unbending, and on the subject of Rhyno van der Bijl he had been *exactly* that. When their previous estate manager had left to buy a place of his own, Kate had begged her father to allow her to take over the management of the estate, but a week later Rhyno had arrived, and Kate had resented him ever since. During the past eighteen months there had not been one thing they had agreed on, and when she had confronted her father on those matters he had merely stated bluntly that Rhyno knew what he was doing.

Kate had quarrelled bitterly with her father on many occasions, but Rhyno van der Bijl had remained firmly instated as estate manager, and he had settled himself comfortably in La Reine's old homestead, the house where he had lived for the first ten years of his life. Kate had not known him then. She had been two years old when Naomi had been forced to sell La Reine and settle in Stellenbosch with her son, but Kate felt certain that she would have disliked him even then.

'My father must have been out of his mind to make such a will!' Kate cried, breaking the tense silence which had settled in the room after Rhyno's abrupt departure, and there was something close to despair in the blue eyes that met Hubert's.

'His mind was perfectly sound, Kate, and you know that as well as I do,' the attorney informed her.

'Aunt Edwina?'

Her hands reached out to the woman who had taken the place of her mother ever since she had been a small child of two, but there was no comfort in the hands that gripped Kate's.

'My dear,' Edwina began gently, 'I don't want Solitaire any more than you want to marry Rhyno, but it wouldn't be wise to come to a hasty decision. Give yourself time—you have almost thirty days, and perhaps, when the shock has worn off, you might not find your father's wishes so unpalatable.'

'I could never marry a man I dislike as intensely as I dislike Rhyno van der Bijl, and besides . . .' Kate paused and withdrew her hands agitatedly from her aunt's, 'there's Gavin.'

'Gavin Page, yes,' Edwina murmured, her lips tightening. 'And where is Gavin today? Why isn't he here to give you the necessary support?'

'He had business to attend to in Cape Town, and he'll only be back tomorrow,' Kate defended the man she had come to care for since their chance meeting three months ago.

Hubert coughed politely. 'Shall we retire to the living-room?'

Edwina nodded, and they rose from the table, their footsteps on the yellow-wood floor echoing across the room.

Naomi van der Bijl awaited them in the spacious living-room with its mixture of modern and antique furnishings. She was seated facing the door, and her dark glance darted towards Rhyno who stood in front of the tall window with his back turned resolutely towards them when they entered. Kate's glance travelled briefly from his proud, dark head down to his polished shoes. His lean body was tanned, and muscled beneath that sober grey suit, and no one knew better than Kate of the strength in those long arms and large rough hands. She had seen him working alongside the labourers in the vineyards when they had been short-staffed, and it was Rhyno who had carried her father single-handed into the house after he had collapsed in the cellars with cardiac arrest.

'I suppose Rhyno has told you?' said Kate, staring down into Naomi van der Bijl's troubled face.

'Yes, and I——'

'I think the least said at this moment, Mother, the better for all of us,' Rhyno interrupted harshly, turning from his contemplation of the garden, and Naomi glanced at him somewhat nervously and nodded.

'Perhaps you're right,' she acknowledged with some reluctance, her hands tightening on her handbag.

'Will you stay and have tea with us, Naomi?' Edwina asked, breaking that short, awkward silence in the room.

'No, thank you,' Naomi shook her head and got to her feet. 'I must think of going home.'

Rhyno stepped forward at once. 'I'll walk you out to your car, Mother, and then there are a few things I have to see to before the afternoon progresses too far.'

Rhyno's abruptness bordered almost on rudeness, and Naomi glanced at him reprovingly before she took her leave of everyone.

Hubert Walton left Solitaire a short while after Naomi van der Bijl, and when Kate found herself alone with her aunt, she cried hoarsely, 'I can't marry that man! *I just can't!*'

'I dare say he feels the same way about you,' Edwina reminded her caustically. 'No man likes to be bulldozed into a marriage he's not ready for.'

'I wish to heaven I knew what had possessed Daddy to make such a ridiculous will,' Kate muttered, pacing the floor agitatedly. 'He *knew* how I felt about that man. Good lord, didn't we have enough arguments during the past

eighteen months to make him realise how much I resented
that man's presence here on Solitaire?'

Edwina smiled reminiscently. 'Your father was always
a shrewd man. He was extremely clever too, but he had
an unpredictable streak in him which made it difficult to
know exactly what to expect of him at times.'

'Lord, don't I know that!' Kate exclaimed, her sapphire
blue eyes flashing as anger and resentment fought for
supremacy. 'I *love* Solitaire. I love every square inch of it,
and I'm *damned* if I'm going to lose what belongs to me!'

'You've made up your mind to marry Rhyno, then?'

'*No!*' Kate retorted fiercely, swinging round to face her
aunt, and her face was set with a mixture of distaste and
determination. 'I'll *never* marry Rhyno, but I'll get
Solitaire somehow.'

When the sun dipped in the west, heralding the start of
a warm January night, a feeling of desolation and despair
replaced the initial shock of hearing the stipulations
Jacques Duval had made in his will. The house was quiet,
too quiet, when Edwina and Kate finally sat down to
dinner in the dining-hall. Her father's chair was empty,
but she felt his presence so distinctly that she could almost
smell the musty odour of the wine cellars which nearly
always clung to his clothes. A lump rose in her throat,
and her eyes filled with tears. She was going to miss him
dreadfully, but mingled with her sorrow was resentment,
anger . . . and bewilderment. If only she could understand
her father's reasons for making those crazy stipulations!

'You're not eating,' Edwina accused, her voice butting
in on Kate's unhappy thoughts.

'I'm not very hungry.'

'You're much too thin,' Edwina complained, her grey
eyes taking in Kate's slenderness in the pale blue dress she
had changed into before dinner. 'And you're not going to
solve your problems by going on a starvation diet.'

Kate raised her glance, and her eyes were clouded as they met those of the grey-haired woman seated opposite her. 'How am I going to solve my problems?'

'You could come to some agreement with Rhyno.'

'Never!' Kate snapped fiercely, her hands clenching on the table.

'He stands to lose just as much as you do,' Edwina reminded her quietly. 'La Reine was once his home, and it's only natural that he would wish to take possession of it again instead of letting it fall into strange hands.'

'Well, that's too bad for him!' Kate replied with unaccustomed callousness. '*Solitaire* is my concern, but I refuse to tie myself to any man in order to get it.'

'How are you going to get Solitaire without marrying Rhyno?' Edwina asked the burning question.

'I don't know.' Kate bit her lip irritably. 'There must be another way. There *has* to be!'

Kate could not fall asleep that night. She lay awake for hours thinking; planning, rejecting, and planning again, but each time she came up against the same blank wall. To take possession of Solitaire she had to marry Rhyno. But what if *he* did not want to marry *her*? She suddenly sat bolt upright in bed. She had not thought of it that way before. What if there was no other way out of this mess, and Rhyno refused?

She shivered despite the warmth of the night, and slipped down beneath the sheet, dragging it up to her chin. There was no reason why Rhyno should want to marry her, except if he wanted La Reine as much as she wanted Solitaire, and not even that would be reason enough. He disliked her as much as she disliked him, and there was no way the two of them could live together peaceably for a year.

'Why do I dislike him so much?' she finally asked herself, and she could not, in all honesty, answer that question. She could not deny that there had been times when she had actually felt attracted to him, and neither could she deny that she had found herself watching him intently on so many occasions when he had been unaware of her presence. There was something indefinable about him which had disturbed her from the first moment they had met all those months ago, but antagonism and conflicting ideas concerning his method of farming had overshadowed everything else, and mostly she had thought of him with resentment; a resentment which had turned to dislike.

Her father had had a very high regard for Rhyno, and there had been times when he had treated him almost like a son. This had puzzled Kate, but she had never questioned her father on the subject. You could argue with Jacques Duval, but one never questioned his actions, for it was something he seldom tolerated. Now he was no longer there; he was lying next to her mother in the shade of the whispering cypress trees, and his actions could not be questioned even if Kate had wanted to.

The slave bell was rung early the following morning to herald the belated start of the harvest, and it was a cool, cloudy day, ideal for picking those swollen, gleaming berries which hung in heavy bunches on the vines. Life had to go on, the production of Solitaire's superb wines had to continue, but Jacques Duval would no longer be there to witness the proceedings. From now until late summer almost every man, woman and child of Solitaire's community would be in the vineyards, filling their baskets as swiftly and deftly as they could. Every basket they filled meant more money in their pockets, and every load that reached the winepress would guarantee the good quality of Solitaire's wines.

Steen . . . Riesling . . . Colombard . . . Kate knew every cultivar grown on Solitaire, she knew their character, and how to blend them, if necessary, for the best results. She had been an apt pupil, eager to learn all there was to know, and always there had been the knowledge that one day Solitaire would belong to her. That dream had now been shattered into tiny fragments. Unless she married Rhyno, or found some escape hole in her father's will, Solitaire would belong to Aunt Edwina with the clear understanding that it would be sold after her death. With Aunt Edwina, however reluctant, at the helm of this large estate, life would go on very much the same as it had done in the past. This was not what troubled Kate. It was the sale of Solitaire after her aunt's eventual death that drove her nearly out of her mind. Strange hands would till the soil, harvest the berries, and nurse the fine wines towards maturity, and those hands might not be as loving as they ought to be.

It was these discomfiting thoughts that made Kate drive into Stellenbosch after lunch that day to see Hubert Walton. She wanted him to read her that last part of her father's will, she wanted to hear every word again to make certain that she had not missed that vital loophole while she had been in a state of shock the previous day, and then, perhaps, she could come to a decision about the future.

When she entered Hubert Walton's office she found Rhyno lounging in a chair with one of his battered pipes clenched between his strong teeth, and the aroma of his particular brand of tobacco was all around her in the smoke-filled room.

'If you've come to find some way out of those confounded stipulations your father made in his will, then you're wasting your time,' Rhyno told her bluntly before Hubert could formulate some sort of welcome. 'Mr Walton and I have spent an exhausting hour going over every detail in your father's will with meticulous care, and there's nothing anyone can do to alter it.'

'I'd like to decide that for myself, thank you,' she told him coldly, resentment stiffening her back, and lighting a spark of antagonism in her eyes.

'Please yourself,' he shrugged, pocketing his pipe and rising to his feet to dominate her with his height, if nothing else. 'When you've satisfied yourself, as I have, that there's no way out, perhaps we could have a serious discussion concerning this awkward matter.'

He nodded abruptly in Hubert's direction, and moments later the panelled door closed behind his tall frame.

'Don't you think you should open a window, Uncle Hubert?' Kate suggested tritely. 'This room positively reeks with his filthy tobacco!'

Hubert raised his heavy eyebrows in faint amusement, but he nevertheless got up behind his desk and opened one of the windows to admit the fresh air. 'Is that better?' he asked blandly.

'Much better,' Kate nodded, still feeling prickly at finding Rhyno there with the attorney.

'Kate,' Hubert began, resuming his seat behind his wide desk, 'if you won't take Rhyno's word for it, then at least take mine. Your father's will is most explicit, and when it was drawn up Jacques made quite sure that his wishes would have to be carried out to the very letter.'

'You mean if I want Solitaire I shall have to marry Rhyno, *if* he'll have me, or I shall have to buy it after Aunt Edwina's death.'

'No bank or building society will give you a loan without the necessary collateral, and if Solitaire should go on the market the price would be beyond most people ... even you, Kate, and the deposit would be phenomenal.'

'But surely I shall have a share in the profits during the years that Solitaire will be in Aunt Edwina's possession?'

Kate questioned sharply. 'Won't there eventually be enough with which to——'

'I shall be handling the financial side, Kate,' Hubert interrupted firmly, 'and I've been instructed to see to it that you and your aunt live comfortably. The rest of whatever profits there are will go into a trust, and it will be added to the money received when Solitaire is sold.'

Kate stiffened and paled considerably. 'You never mentioned this yesterday.'

'No, I didn't mention it,' Hubert admitted calmly, 'and I withheld this information for the simple reason that I was hoping you and Rhyno would be able to work something out together.'

'You mean you're actually hoping that I'll marry him?' she asked incredulously, lowering herself into the chair Rhyno had vacated some minutes before, and she stared at the attorney as if she thought he had gone mad.

'I'm hoping,' Hubert said, 'that you'll give the situation a great deal of sensible thought, and I'm hoping that you love Solitaire enough to want to keep it.'

The intercom buzzed on his desk, and when he flicked the required switch his secretary's voice said: 'Mr Baxter is here to see you, Mr Walton.'

'Ask him to wait a moment, will you?'

Hubert flicked that same switch and raised his glance apologetically, but Kate was already on her feet, her handbag clutched tightly under her arm.

'It was kind of you to see me without an appointment, and I must be going,' she said quickly, disappointment etched in the curve of her mouth. 'I have a lot to think about.'

She walked out of his office and took the lift down to the ground floor. Slim and elegant in her cinnamon-coloured suit, she was unaware of the admiring glances following her as she crossed the street to where she had parked her Mercedes sports car which had been a gift from her father on her last birthday. She had too much to think about, and her mind was in too much of a turmoil to be aware of anything that went on around her at that moment.

'Kate!' A hand gripped her arm, and a startled gasp escaped her as she found herself staring up into Rhyno's dark, unfathomable eyes. 'We have to talk, and the sooner we do so, the better.'

'We have nothing to say to each other,' she argued stubbornly, trying to extricate her arm from his steel-like grip, but his fingers merely tightened, biting into the soft flesh until she was forced to cease her efforts.

'There's a bench over there beneath the trees,' he said, gesturing with his free hand. 'We'll talk there.'

His dominating attitude infuriated her, but a busy pavement in the centre of town was not the place for a scene, and she allowed herself to be led towards the bench with an audible sigh of resignation which lit a spark of anger in his eyes.

CHAPTER TWO

'You may let go of my arm,' Kate said icily when she was seated beside Rhyno on the wooden bench, and although he released her at once she had the distinct feeling that she was as much a prisoner as before. His lean, muscled body was ready for action at a moment's notice if she should try to escape, and she knew that it would be futile to try.

'I know we haven't always agreed in the past, but I think we've always managed to be civil to each other.'

Kate flashed him an angry glance. 'Get to the point!'

'Don't treat me as if I dictated your father's will.' His eyes were hard, and his mouth was drawn into a thin, ruthless line. 'We're in the same boat, you and I, and we'll just have to make the best of things. We have time to consider what we're going to do, but that's the only thing we have time for at the moment. The harvest must go on, and without your father there to help me I'm finding it difficult trying to be in two places at the same time.'

Her soft, pink lips curved in a cynical smile. 'Are you asking me to help you?'

'Why not?' His mouth twitched and relaxed slightly. 'Despite your old-fashioned ideas you have an outstanding knowledge of winemaking, and your assistance now during the harvest season could be a valuable asset.'

'Really?'

'Sarcasm doesn't suit you, Kate,' he rebuked her sharply. 'Will you help me?'

'Yes,' she snapped bitterly. 'Although I don't know why

25

I should. Between you and my father you did your level best to exclude me from everything except the paper work during the past year and a half, and now I'm suddenly good enough to take my father's place.'

'Until you decide one way or the other, Kate, Solitaire is yours,' he reminded her harshly. 'Let me down now, and in the end you'll be letting Solitaire down.'

Kate winced inwardly and avoided those dark, penetrating eyes. 'You certainly know how to hit below the belt, don't you?'

'Someone has to bring you to your senses.'

'And you consider you're the one to do it?'

'If I have to do it, then I will,' he stated bluntly. 'We can't all spend our days feeling sorry for you, Kate.'

'Feeling sorry for me?' She almost choked on the words, and anger sparkled in the eyes that met his. 'How dare you!'

'It's the truth, whether you like it or not,' Rhyno insisted blandly. 'Hubert Walton and your Aunt Edwina are both too sorry for you to tell you to snap out of it. The future has to be faced, and you can't face it with a head full of woolly notions. When you want something you have to work for it, and that goes for Solitaire as well. If you want the estate, then you will have to prove that you're worthy of it.'

Her angry glance did not waver from his as she asked cynically, 'How badly do you want La Reine?'

His expression hardened ruthlessly. 'I want it badly enough to consider marrying you for it.'

'Over my dead body will you get La Reine that way!' she exclaimed fiercely, her insides in revolt at the mere thought of marrying this man.

'I think we should get back to the estate. There's work to be done, and we're wasting precious daylight,' he said, and his seemingly unperturbed manner merely infuriated her more, but she bit back the angry words that rose to her lips as he drew her to her feet and accompanied her to where she had parked her car.

Rhyno followed her all the way to Solitaire in the estate truck as if he didn't trust her to go straight home. Abominable man! When she arrived at the house she changed quickly into an old pair of jeans, a blue and white chequered blouse, and comfortable shoes, then she left the house and walked briskly down to the cellars.

The winepresses were working fast and furiously to keep up with the amount of grapes being brought in on loaded trailers; white grapes from Solitaire, and the black Cabernet Sauvignon, Cinsaut and Pinotage from La Reine. They were all top quality wine cultivars, and the steel fermentation tanks were being filled again before the long process of maturation began.

Kate took over her father's tasks automatically without Rhyno having to instruct her what to do. While he was at La Reine to supervise the harvesting, she would keep an eye on the cellars and the vineyards on Solitaire. She checked the machinery, rectified a belt that was faulty, and issued a few brief instructions before driving herself down to the vineyards in the dusty estate jeep.

There was no laughter in the vineyards on the day after Jacques Duval's burial, but the pickers sang while they worked even though the songs had an unmistakable ring of sadness to them. Kate watched them work for a while, marvelling as always at the deftness of their hands as the ripe bunches of grapes were transferred from the vines to their baskets. When a tractor towed away a loaded trailer, an empty trailer arrived on cue. The farm hands knew what they were doing; they had done the same thing year after year, and they worked with a precision and timing which could seldom be faulted.

'We're going to have a good crop this year, Miss Kate.

One of the best,' they assured her, and by 'good crop' they did not mean quantity but quality.

She drove back to the wine cellars where she knew she would be needed most. It was late afternoon when the last load of grapes arrived and was tipped into the wine-press, but tomorrow, at the first light of day, it would start all over again, and it would go on day after day until all the berries had been harvested.

'We've made a good start,' Rhyno assured her when he looked in on the wine cellar. 'I think your father would have been pleased.'

Kate nodded and turned away, too choked suddenly to speak at his reference to her father. She checked that everything was in order, then she walked out into the fresh air, away from the smell of crushed grapes, and away from Rhyno who seemed to be watching her with a brooding expression on his face that disturbed her.

Gavin Page arrived at Solitaire that evening after dinner, and Aunt Edwina immediately took herself off to some other part of the house. She had never made a secret of the fact that she did not approve of Kate's friendship with Gavin, and Kate had been only too aware that her father had shared his sister's views, but that did not deter her from seeing Gavin and making up her own mind about him.

'I'm sorry I couldn't be here yesterday,' Gavin apologised when she led the way into the living-room.

'It doesn't matter,' she assured him with an unnatural airiness. 'There was nothing you could do anyway.'

Gavin was only slightly taller than Kate, with dark brown hair, and laughing blue eyes in his angular face, but his eyes were not laughing at that moment as he studied her intently. 'Are you all right?'

'I'm fine,' she said breezily. 'Just fine.'

'I missed you.'

'Oh, Gavin!' she sighed, the tension easing within her, and she went into his arms without waiting for an invitation. 'Hold me, and tell me this is all a bad dream.'

'Darling, don't upset yourself,' he frowned, tightening his arms about her when he realised that she was crying. 'I can't bear to see you like this.'

'I'm sorry,' she muttered with a touch of cynicism in her smile as she drew away from him to brush away her tears with the tips of her fingers. 'Rhyno was right—I really should pull myself together.'

Gavin's mouth tightened. 'Has that man been making life difficult for you?'

'It's not Rhyno who's making life difficult for me, it's my father.'

'Your father?' Gavin frowned. 'I don't think I understand.'

She gestured vaguely with her hands. 'It doesn't matter, and I don't really want to talk about it.'

'What you need, my darling Kate, is someone to take care of you.'

'Are you asking me to marry you?' she teased lightly, allowing him to draw her down on to the sofa and into his arms.

'Why not?' he smiled confidently. 'Together we could make Solitaire the best wine estate in the country, and not just in this area.'

'Solitaire,' Kate murmured soberly. 'It's funny how everything lately seems to revolve around Solitaire.'

'Kate?'

'Oh, there's La Reine too, we mustn't forget that,' she added bitterly.

'Darling, what's the matter?'

'Do you know what solitaire means?' she asked him, despair lurking in her eyes and in the slight smile curving her mouth. 'It means solitary, lonely, and God knows I've never felt more lonely and lost in all my life.'

'Don't say that, Kate,' he ordered, rubbing his cheek against her forehead. 'I'm here with you, aren't I?'

'I'm sorry, Gavin. I'm not actually pleasant company this evening.'

His arms tightened about her. 'Darling, I know this isn't the time to talk about it, but you will marry me, won't you?'

Kate would have given anything to be able to say 'yes' at that moment, but she dared not. If she married Gavin she would lose Solitaire, and a horrible little voice asked her whether Gavin was worthy of such a sacrifice.

'Let's not think of marriage yet, Gavin,' she said hastily, shutting her mind to the disturbing thoughts racing through it. 'Let's simply go on enjoying each other's company for a little while longer.'

Gavin did not look altogether happy, but he nodded agreeably, and moved a little away from her to light a cigarette. 'Meet me in town for lunch tomorrow?'

'I'm afraid I can't,' she said, watching him blow a cloud of smoke towards the beamed ceiling. 'I'm helping with the harvest, and we'll be busy most of the day.'

'I don't see why you should help when you have a manager to see to things,' Gavin scowled.

'There's La Reine as well as Solitaire, Gavin, and keeping an eye on two farms is more than one person can cope with during the harvest season,' she reluctantly defended Rhyno.

'You can afford to take on an extra man, so why don't you get someone to help?' Gavin argued, but she shook her head firmly.

'That's out of the question at the moment.'

'But——'

'Please, Gavin,' she interrupted tiredly, 'could we talk about something else?'

He stared down at the cigarette smouldering between his fingers with a faintly dissatisfied expression on his face, then he raised his glance and sighed resignedly. 'If you can't have lunch with me tomorrow, then what about having dinner with me tomorrow evening?'

'I'd like that,' she said, brushing a long, silky strand of hair away from her face, and Gavin leaned forward at once to kiss her on her smiling lips.

Kate steered the conversation away from herself after that, and questioned Gavin about his work at the winery in Stellenbosch. He needed very little encouragement in that direction, and her interest in winemaking made her a knowledgeable listener. It helped to talk about something else, and for the next hour she could almost shed her problems.

When Gavin eventually drove away from Solitaire, the stark reality of Kate's situation returned with a vengeance to the surface of her mind, and she went to bed feeling depressed. The future lay like a dense jungle ahead of her. There was only one path through it, but she refused to take it and, with a stubbornness she had inherited from her father, she clung to that decision.

She was up at dawn the following morning, and was snatching a quick breakfast in the kitchen when Rhyno arrived. She heard him talking to Aunt Edwina in the hall and, hoping to avoid him, she swallowed down the remainder of her coffee and darted out the back way.

The jeep was not where she had parked it the night before, and she was looking about for it a little wildly when she saw Rhyno striding purposefully towards her.

'Good morning,' he said abruptly with a faint gleam of mockery in his eyes as if he was well aware of the fact that she had tried to avoid him. 'I'll give you a lift down to the cellars.'

'That's not necessary,' she told him coldly. 'The jeep is here somewhere.'

'The jeep was needed on La Reine, and I had it collected earlier this morning.'

'How dare you take it without consulting me first?' she demanded, rounding on him furiously.

'The jeep is not your private property, Kate. It belongs to the estate, and it's used where it's needed most.'

He was right, *damn* him, and right that minute she hated him for it, but she was not given the opportunity to say more. Strong fingers were gripping her arm firmly, and she was steered unceremoniously towards the truck parked a little distance away.

Kate stole a glance at his profile when she was seated beside him in the cab of the sturdy truck, and his beak-like nose with the stern mouth and unrelenting jaw made her realise once again that his sunbronzed features could have been carved out of granite. He was not a man one would associate with any tender, passionate feelings, and yet he was constantly in the company of Barbara Owen who owned one of those exclusive boutiques in Stellenbosch. Were they lovers? Kate blushed at the thought and looked away, shutting her mind to it. It was none of her business, after all, what kind of relationship Rhyno had with this woman.

'I'll pick you up again at twelve,' Rhyno said when he dropped her off at the cellars, and before she could reply he was driving away with the rugged tyres of the truck kicking up a cloud of dust.

When the tractor pulling the first loaded trailer came up the track towards the cellars, Kate gave Lenny the signal to start the machines, and his brown face glowed with that expectancy and excitement which one experienced only at this time of the year. Lenny had seen many summers come and go on Solitaire, but each year, he had told her once, was a new adventure. When the winepress

ceased its function at the end of the harvest one was left
to wonder whether this year's vintage would be a good
one. Would it live up to Solitaire's usual gold medal stand-
ards, or would it receive a lower rating? There was
always that element of surprise; that something to work
for and look forward to, and when your year's labour was
rewarded with success it stirred up a fire in your veins
which no wine could put there. Lenny was good at des-
cribing things, Kate recalled now as she worked alongside him. He had said that once the excitement of winemaking was in your blood, there was nothing on this earth
that could rid you of it, and Kate knew this to be
true.

Helping with the harvest possessed its own kind of ther-
apy, Kate soon discovered. There was little time to think,
and even less time to brood, but when Rhyno picked her
up at twelve, as he had promised, it brought everything
sharply into focus once more. She could never marry this
cold, heartless man; not even if he went down on his knees
and begged her to!

She had lunch with Aunt Edwina in the small dining-
room directly off the kitchen. She ate sparsely, not wanting to return to work on a full stomach, and declined the
cup of tea her aunt offered her, settling instead for a glass
of iced water.

'I've invited Rhyno to have dinner with us this evening,' Aunt Edwina made her surprise announcement while
she calmly added milk and sugar to her tea.

'I'm afraid the two of you will be dining alone,' Kate
informed her at once. 'I'm dining out with Gavin this
evening.'

'You could have told me sooner,' her aunt complained,
and Kate shrugged carelessly.

'I could have, I suppose, but it slipped my mind.'

'Well, it's too late to retract my invitation, so I can

only hope Rhyno won't object to an old woman's company at dinner.'

'I'm sure the two of you will have a lot to talk about,' Kate smiled cynically, glad now that she had accepted Gavin's invitation.

'And what's that supposed to mean?' Aunt Edwina demanded, her reproving glance sweeping over Kate.

'You've always liked him, haven't you?'

'I was fond of him when he was a little boy, and I find him utterly charming as a man.'

'Charming!' Kate snorted, almost choking on a mouthful of water. 'There's nothing charming about Rhyno van der Bijl. He's an arrogant, self-opinionated and boorish individual who possesses about as much refinement as that cheap, obnoxious wine some of the workers like to drink.'

'Kate!' Aunt Edwina gasped admonishingly, her glance darting beyond her niece. 'You should guard your tongue!'

'It pays sometimes to know exactly what other people think of you, Aunt Edwina,' Rhyno spoke almost directly behind Kate, making her jump, and she swung round on her chair to glare up at·him.

'You know what they say about people who listen at keyholes,' she said bitingly.

'They seldom hear good of themselves, I know,' he nodded, his disparaging glance sliding over her in a way that fanned the fire of her anger and resentment. 'If you're not too refined to soil those lily-white hands of yours, then I suggest we get back to work,' he ordered harshly.

Flames of fury leapt in Kate's eyes. 'Just who do you think you're speaking to?'

'I'm speaking to you, Kate Duval, now get off that butt of yours and let's get some work done.'

She reacted instinctively, her fingers tightening on her

glass, and the next instant its contents were running in little rivulets down his tanned face and dripping on to his blue shirt.

'Kate!' Aunt Edwina's disapproving voice sliced through the electrifying silence in the room. 'What on earth has got into you!'

'Could I please have your table napkin, Aunt Edwina?' Rhyno asked without taking his eyes off Kate, who sat staring up at him with a mixture of defiance and horror in her blue eyes.

'Yes, of course,' Aunt Edwina replied hastily, placing the square of white damask in his outstretched hand.

'Dry my face,' he instructed in a clipped voice, almost thrusting the table napkin in Kate's face.

'Dry it yourself!' she snapped defiantly, but she regretted it the next instant when his fingers snaked about her wrist, and she was jerked up out of her chair to stand so close to him that she could almost feel the disturbing heat of his body through her clothes.

'You will dry my face, or I'll put you across my knee and give you the spanking you deserve.'

'You wouldn't dare!' she hissed, throwing back her head so that her hair fell like a pale, silken cloud down her slim back.

'Don't tempt me, Kate,' he warned softly, and there was something in those dark eyes burning down into hers that warned her not to drive him too far in this respect.

'Give me that thing,' she snapped furiously, conscious of Aunt Edwina's silent, disapproving appraisal as she snatched the table napkin from his hand and dried his chiselled features. He watched her intently while she repaired the damage she had caused and, unnerved, she flung the napkin on to the table when she was finished. 'Satisfied?' she asked coldly.

'For the moment, yes,' he informed her with equal

coldness, his fingers still biting into her tender flesh about
her wrist. 'Now, let's get back to work.'

Helpless fury raged through Kate, but she gritted her
teeth and remained silent as he literally dragged her out
of the house. She would still get the opportunity to speak
her mind, and then she would tell him exactly what she
thought of him!

The hours passed swiftly, and when Kate arrived home
late that afternoon, she bathed and washed the dust out
of her hair. She dressed with care that evening, selecting
a rose-coloured silk evening dress which made her look
and feel good, and her efforts were rewarded when she
was seated opposite Gavin in the quiet little restaurant
where he had taken her so often before.

Across the candlelit table Gavin's blue gaze rested on
her appreciatively. 'You look lovely this evening, Kate.'

'Thank you,' she smiled. 'My morale needs a bit of a
boost, I must say.'

'I didn't say that merely to boost your morale,' he assured
her at once, clasping her hand across the table. 'I meant it,'
he added, 'and I only wish you were wearing my ring.'

Kate eyed him a little warily. 'Don't get serious, Gavin.'

'I want to marry you, Kate.' His fingers tightened about
hers when she would have drawn her hand away. 'We've
known each other long enough, and now is the time that
you need a man out there at Solitaire to help you keep
things in order.'

'Rhyno is there,' she replied cautiously.

'But he's only the estate manager, Kate,' Gavin protested. 'You *own* the estate now, and I can't see Rhyno
van der Bijl taking orders from a woman.'

'I don't own Solitaire, Gavin,' she said, bitterness rising
sharply within her. 'Not yet anyway.'

He gestured impatiently. 'I realise that there's still the
legal side of it to be seen to, but you were your father's

sole heir, so you can justifiably say that the estate belongs to you.'

'It will take time before I can say that,' she smiled wryly.

'A few months, I agree,' he shrugged off her statement.

'A year, or perhaps a little less than a month,' she corrected him thoughtfully.

Gavin studied her intently for a moment, then he laughed shortly. 'I'm afraid you've lost me.'

'May I have a little more wine?' she asked, pushing her glass across the table towards him.

'Certainly,' he smiled, releasing her hand and filling up her glass, but that eager light in his eyes died swiftly when his glance met hers again. 'What's troubling you, Kate?'

'You are,' she replied honestly, taking a sip of her wine and comparing the quality subconsciously with Solitaire's. 'I want to forget about Solitaire, and the problems my father has left behind for me to deal with, but you insist on dragging it into the conversation.'

'If there are problems, then surely I could help you sort them out?' he offered eagerly.

'I'm afraid you can't.' Her eyes clouded. 'I'm the only one who could sort out the mess I'm in at the moment, but when I'm with you I would very much like to forget about everything, and simply relax.'

'Very well, I accept that, but——' He smiled, but his smile was no longer as confident as before. 'If there's ever anything I could assist you with, you will let me know, won't you? After all, I do have an interest in you, and therefore in Solitaire, not so?'

Kate swallowed down the lump in her throat, and nodded. 'I appreciate your interest and your concern, Gavin, and I shall remember your offer of assistance.'

'Shall we order?' he asked when the waiter appeared beside their table with the menu.

'Yes, please,' she smiled, aware of that uncomfortable hollow at the pit of her stomach. 'I am rather hungry.'

Gavin did not mention marriage, nor Solitaire again, but he did speak often of starting his own computer firm if he could acquire a partner who would be willing to buy himself into the business. Computers were *the* thing these days, Gavin had explained enthusiastically, and if Kate had had more than just her allowance, she would have considered going into partnership with him, but under the circumstances it was impossible, so she remained no more than an avid listener to his plans.

As the days lengthened into weeks Kate's life seemed to follow a certain pattern. She worked hard during the day, and most evenings she dined with Gavin, or went out to a show with him. Her weekends, too, were spent with Gavin, and they would go for long drives into the picturesque countryside to enjoy a picnic somewhere. Occasionally they spent the day at Solitaire, swimming, or having a game of tennis, but Kate preferred not to remain where she could run into Rhyno at any moment to have her memory jolted back to the things she wanted to forget.

Aunt Edwina disapproved of Kate's behaviour, and made no secret of the fact, but for the first time in Kate's life she paid no heed to her aunt's reprimands. Gavin was an entertaining companion, and when she was with him she somehow managed to shake off her disturbing thoughts.

Gavin drove her home one evening after they had been out to dinner and a show, and when he parked his car in Solitaire's circular driveway, she turned in her seat to face him.

'I won't ask you in, Gavin,' she said softly. 'It's late, and I'm rather tired.'

'I'll see you tomorrow evening, then,' he replied, drawing her into his arms and kissing her lingeringly on the mouth.

His lips were passionate as always, and tiredness made her respond with more warmth than she had intended. Gavin was instantly aware of this, and he drew her closer into his embrace, but when his hand came to rest against the side of her breast she hastily extricated herself from his arms and, fumbling for the handle of the door in the darkness, she murmured a quick 'goodnight'.

Gavin did not attempt to stop her from leaving the car, and when she ran lightly up the steps she heard him drive away.

Solitaire's Gothic gables stood etched against the starry sky, and there was not a light on in the house as Kate quickened her step to reach the heavy oak door. The scent of honeysuckle mingled with that of the roses and gardenias, but when she inserted the key in the latch her sensitive nose detected the pungent and familiar aroma of tobacco in the night air, and she did not need to be told who was emerging from the shadows of the tall hibiscus.

'What are you doing here?' she asked sharply, her eyes straining in the darkness to see Rhyno clearly.

'I had dinner with your aunt and stayed on to keep her company, but when she went to bed I decided to hang around until you returned home.'

'Don't tell me you've decided to install yourself as a guard dog now,' she laughed sarcastically when he stood directly in front of her.

'Do you think it's wise to stay out this late every evening when you have to be up at dawn the next morning?' he asked tersely, ignoring her remark.

'I've always been an early riser no matter what hours I keep.'

'I accept that,' he replied blandly, 'but then you

haven't always had to put in a hard day's work after a
heavy date the night before, have you.'

Kate stiffened with resentment. 'If you've expected me
to be slack on the job, then I'm sorry I've disappointed
you.'

'It's not your slackness on the job that troubles me, it's
your health,' he contradicted harshly. 'You can't burn
the candle at both ends, Kate, and that's what you've
been doing these past three weeks.'

'Don't concern yourself,' she snapped up at him, the
moonlight glinting in her angry eyes. 'I know what I'm
doing.'

'Do you?' he queried with a mixture of condescension
and mockery in his voice that infuriated her more.

'I don't interfere in your life, Rhyno van der Bijl, so
don't interfere in mine!'

That would have been a perfect exit line, but when she
would have turned away his hands shot out and gripped
her shoulders firmly.

'Time is running out,' he reminded her bluntly, 'and
we have to come to some sort of decision about the
future.'

'To *hell* with the future!' she spat out the words fiercely,
and when his hands tightened on her shoulders she bit
back a cry of pain.

'That's not you talking, Kate,' he said harshly. 'You
love Solitaire too much to turn your back on it and say to
hell with it.'

'*Take your hands off me!*'

To her surprise he removed his hands, but he did not
move away from her, but stood there towering over her in
the darkness, dominating her with his height and the
breadth of his shoulders.

'Stay home tomorrow evening so that we can discuss
what's to be done,' he suggested, but Kate flung back her

head and stared up into his shadowed face defiantly.

'I'm going out tomorrow evening, *and* the evening after that, and I shan't be home the weekend either. I'm going to Cape Town with Gavin to spend a few days with some friends of his.'

'You're not being fair, Kate,' Rhyno accused. 'You're not being fair to your aunt, you're not being fair to me, but most of all you're not being fair to Solitaire.'

'Solitaire!' she repeated cynically, her hands clutching her evening purse so tightly that her fingers ached. 'It's not Solitaire you're concerned about, Rhyno, it's *La Reine*. You just can't wait to get your greedy hands on La Reine, but the only way you can get it is through me, and I'm damned if I'll be used as your stepping stone!'

She heard him draw a sharp breath, and the ensuing silence was suddenly dangerously explosive. She had perhaps gone too far, but she was beyond caring at that moment. He could do as he pleased, but nothing would induce her to change her mind.

'We'll discuss this matter again when you're in a more sensible frame of mind,' he said at length with a coldness in his voice which would have chilled her had she not been in such a red-hot fury.

'Not if I can help it!' she bit out the words, but he had already turned on his heel and was striding away to become one with the shadows.

Alone in her room, when her anger had subsided, Kate experienced a twinge of shame, but that made no difference to how she felt about the whole miserable business. She was well aware that there was only a week left in which to decide what to do, but she dared not think about it. Working on Solitaire during the past weeks had, however, taught her one thing, and that was that she loved it too much to let it go. The solution was simple; all she had to do was marry Rhyno and stay married to him for a year, but the thought of becoming his wife sent a shiver of distaste up her spine.

The whole thing was ridiculous from start to finish, she told herself. It was like those games she had played as a child when one had to pay a forfeit for some reason or other. In this instance marrying Rhyno was the forfeit, and the prize attached to it was Solitaire.

Solitaire; her love and her life from those days when she had sat on her father's broad shoulders as he walked through the vineyards, pointing out the different cultivars, and explaining the intricate process of winemaking even though she had been too young at the time to grasp it all.

She could not let Solitaire go, but she would not give in to her father's atrocious demands without a struggle.

CHAPTER THREE

THE clock on the mantelshelf chimed seven-thirty. Gavin was late, Kate thought anxiously as she watched Aunt Edwina's knitting needles flashing in the light of the reading lamp. If Gavin did not arrive soon they would miss part of the show they were going to see, and nothing annoyed her more than arriving late and having to find her way about in the semi-darkness while people objected loudly to having their view obstructed.

A car approached the house, but Kate knew the sound of Rhyno's old Citroën too well to mistake it for Gavin's gleaming Peugeot, and her insides quivered with apprehension.

'I wonder what Rhyno wants?' Kate asked when her aunt looked up from her knitting, but Edwina merely shrugged slightly and continued knitting until the end of that row.

A car door slammed, and moments later Rhyno was entering the house as though he owned it, his footsteps muted on the carpeted floor of the entrance hall as he crossed it and approached the living-room.

'Good evening, Aunt Edwina ... Kate,' he nodded in her direction as he entered the room, and for some obscure reason her pulses behaved oddly as she sensed the whipcord strength of his lean body.

Aunt Edwina muttered something that escaped Kate at that moment and, gathering up her knitting, she walked out of the living-room, leaving Kate and Rhyno alone.

His white, short-sleeved shirt stretched tightly across his wide shoulders, and a broad leather belt hugged his brown

pants to his slim hips, but Kate's glance was drawn irrevocably to those compelling eyes beneath straight dark
brows.

'If you've come to discuss something with me, then
you're wasting your time. I'm expecting Gavin at any
moment,' she broke the prolonged silence in the room.

'Gavin won't be coming this evening,' Rhyno informed
her, taking a packet of cigarettes out of the top pocket of
his shirt, and lighting one as he stepped farther into the
room. 'I took the liberty of letting him know that you
couldn't make it.'

Anger choked her as she rose from her chair, and her
silk wrap fell unnoticed to the floor as she faced Rhyno
across the space dividing them. 'How *dare* you do such a
thing, you—you——'

'Calling me names isn't going to solve anything, Kate,'
he interrupted smoothly, his narrowed eyes on her face as
he drew hard on his cigarette.

'I hate you!'

'I'm sure you do,' he replied with that infuriating
calmness as he bent to pick up her wrap, 'but you know
as well as I do that you have a responsibility towards
everything your father has achieved here on Solitaire, and
no matter how much you hate me, you're going to have
to face it.'

'You really want La Reine badly, don't you?' she spat
out the words as she snatched her wrap from his fingers
and flung it on to the chair behind her. 'I dare say you've
spent the past eighteen months ingratiating yourself with
my father in the hope that he would leave La Reine to
you, and you succeeded, didn't you, but, like myself, you
never bargained for the conditions attached to this inheritance.'

Rhyno's glance did not falter and, except for a slight
tightening of his mouth, his expression remained the same.

•

'All I've ever wanted was the opportunity to work on the farm which was my birthplace. Inheriting La Reine never entered into my plans, but now that it has I'm determined that it shan't fall into strange hands, and if it would make you happy, then I shall pay you for it some day when I'm in a position to do so.'

The fire ebbed from Kate's eyes, and she turned away from him abruptly to hide her shame. She felt mean and petty, and disgusted with herself. None of what she had said was true. She had intended to hurt him, but she had succeeded only in shaming herself.

'I don't want to marry you,' she said in a relatively calm voice while she kept her back turned rigidly towards him.

'Do you think I enjoy the thought of being forced into marriage?'

She shook her head and sighed. 'No, I don't suppose you do.'

'Then we at least agree on something.'

'Oh, it's all so grossly unfair!' she exclaimed, her eyes sparkling with renewed fury and frustration as she swung round to face him again, and with her arms wrapped almost protectively about herself she paced the floor very much like a caged animal.

Rhyno watched her for a moment while he smoked his cigarette in silence, then he lowered himself into a chair and said mockingly, 'You won't achieve anything by wearing out the carpet in that way.'

'All right,' she snapped, pausing in her stride to face him. 'If you're so clever then let's have a few suggestions.'

'Before I make any suggestions there are a few facts I'd like to establish.' Twin jets of smoke came from his nostrils, making him look like the devil himself, then he crushed his cigarette into the ashtray and stretched his long legs out before him. 'You asked me how badly I want La

Reine, and I've told you, but now I'm asking you—how badly do you want Solitaire?'

Kate stared at him from across the room, her small, rounded chin set with determination, and her generous mouth tightening. 'I'd rather die than let it eventually go to strangers.'

'Right!' He motioned her into her chair, and she obeyed like someone without a will of her own. 'Now we're at last on an equal footing. You want Solitaire, and I want La Reine.'

'Clever!' she bit out the word sarcastically. 'That still leaves us with marriage as the only way out.'

'Substitute the words "business arrangement" for "marriage", and you might find the idea more palatable.'

Kate's hands gripped the arms of her chair. 'A business arrangement?'

'Yes,' he nodded, a faint smile curving his hard mouth. 'What it amounts to is a legal arrangement which will be binding for a year. When that year is up we have the arrangement declared null and void, and we part company, but this time you'll have what you want, and the same will apply for myself.'

'When you say it like that it sounds so simple, doesn't it?' she laughed shortly.

'It *is* very simple and straightforward.'

She gestured impatiently. 'No matter how much you camouflage it, it still means marriage, and marriage to you means making a pretence of living together for the stipulated period.'

'Isn't Solitaire worth the sacrifice?'

'Damn you, Rhyno, of course it is, but——' She was on her feet again, pacing the floor as if her life depended on it. 'I shall have to think it over.'

'You haven't much time for that,' he reminded her coldly. 'We have less than a week.'

'I'll give you my answer after the weekend.'

'I'm afraid that's not good enough,' Rhyno replied abruptly, and her eyes flew to his as he got to his feet.

'What do you mean that's not good enough?' she demanded with a suffocating tightness in her chest.

'Don't play games, Kate,' he admonished her harshly. 'I've given you ample opportunity to meet me half way, but you've remained stubborn. You know as well as I do that there's only one way out of this situation, so there's no point in spinning it out until the very last minute.'

She eyed him suspiciously. 'You sound as if you have everything arranged and waiting solely for my signature.'

'As a matter of fact, I have,' he confirmed blandly. 'We have a harvest in progress on the estate, and neither of us can afford to waste time during the week for the necessary ceremony, so I've made arrangements for us to be married on Saturday morning.'

'Well, you'll just have to cancel the arrangements, won't you?' she said icily, shaking inwardly with anger.

'I'll cancel nothing!' he barked at her, his tight-lipped expression ominous as he breached the gap between them to tower over her. 'You marry me Saturday morning or you lose Solitaire, and that's final!'

A cold hand gripped her heart, but her smile was cynical as she stared up into his dark, thunderous eyes. 'Don't forget it would also mean that you would lose La Reine.'

'I'd rather lose La Reine than sacrifice myself on the altar of a woman's whims.'

She winced inwardly and that coldness spread from her heart through into her veins. She knew him well enough to know that he had meant every word he had said, and the situation was suddenly humiliatingly clear. *She* was the one who was desperate, but not for anything in the world would she let him see this.

'It seems as though I don't have much of a choice,' she finally broke the strained silence.

'You've never had a choice, Kate, and neither have I,' Rhyno stated with such bitterness in his voice that she experienced the oddest desire to reach out and comfort him, but she suppressed it instantly when he continued speaking. 'Your father knew what he was doing when he drew up that will. He knew how much these farms meant to us, but heaven only knows what he hoped to achieve by adding those impossible stipulations.'

'If he had some crazy idea that we would eventually decide to continue with our marriage, then he was mistaken,' she almost spat out the words with renewed anger. 'I don't intend to stay married to you a day longer than is absolutely necessary.'

'Those are my sentiments exactly.'

His cold, clipped voice seemed to drain the breath from her lungs, and she turned away from him as she said dully, 'Then I'm sure we understand each other perfectly.'

'Perfectly,' he echoed abruptly.

Kate took a deep breath to steady herself before she turned to face him. 'Was there anything else you wished to discuss with me?'

'There is one other matter,' he nodded, lighting another cigarette and taking his time about it. 'What have you told your boy-friend?'

Her back stiffened involuntarily. 'I've told Gavin nothing.'

'You'll be seeing him tomorrow evening, and I would like to suggest that you keep it that way when you tell him that you're going to marry me.'

'Oh, I'm going to be allowed to see him again, am I?' she asked sarcastically.

'For the last time, yes,' Rhyno nodded abruptly. 'I intend that our marriage should appear to be a real one, except of course to those immediately involved, such as Hubert Walton, my mother, and your aunt.'

She stared at him aghast. 'You mean we're going to have to put on a show of affection in public?'

'I shan't expect you to walk around looking starry-eyed and lovesick,' he replied, his mouth twisting cynically, 'but I shall expect of you a certain civility which will give the impression that our marriage was entered into for the usual reasons.'

Her eyes, cold like chips of ice, met his. 'Was there anything else?'

'Yes,' he said abruptly, blowing a stream of smoke towards the ceiling. 'When you see Gavin tomorrow evening, you will say what you have to say, then you will see to it that he brings you home at a reasonable hour.'

His dictatorial manner infuriated her, and with her hands clenched at her sides she snapped at him, 'Get out, Rhyno, before I throw something at you!'

'Sleep well, Kate,' he smiled cynically, and moments later she was alone in the vast living-room with its memories of evenings spent there with her father.

Oh, how she wished he was there at that moment! She would give him a piece of her mind, and she would most certainly break the golden rule by demanding to know exactly what he had had in mind by attaching so many strings to her inheritance.

'Kate?'

Aunt Edwina had come into the living-room so quietly that Kate had not heard her.

'We're going to be married on Saturday,' Kate replied to her silent query and, afraid suddenly that she was going to burst into ridiculous tears, she brushed past her aunt and practically ran to her room.

Kate dreaded having to confront Gavin with the news of

her coming marriage to Rhyno. All through the following day she could think of nothing else, and as the hours passed she became tense with the knowledge of what lay ahead of her. She saw Rhyno only briefly during that day, and it was just as well that he stayed out of her way, for she was in the perfect mood to make him the target of her frustration and anger.

That evening, facing Gavin across the table in the restaurant they usually frequented, she could not bring herself to break the news to him. He was relating so eagerly the plans he had made for the weekend they were to spend with his friends in Cape Town that she did not have the heart to burst the bubble of his excitement, and the evening wore on without him noticing her unenthusiastic responses.

A glance at her wrist watch finally made her eyes widen in alarm. It was after eleven, and she could no longer delay the inevitable.

'Gavin, there's something I must tell you. I . . .' She faltered nervously and, her carefully prepared speech forgotten, she plunged in at the deep end. 'I can't go away with you to your friends this weekend.'

Gavin stared at her with a mixture of surprise and annoyance. 'But everything is arranged, and they're expecting us!'

'I'm sorry.' She looked away guiltily, and gathered her flagging courage about her. 'I'm marrying Rhyno tomorrow.'

Gavin stared at her for a moment with a look of shocked incredulity on his angular face, then he laughed loudly. 'Don't be silly, Kate!'

'It's the truth,' she said, lowering her voice when she became aware of the curious glances directed at them. 'I'm marrying him tomorrow morning.'

He leaned his elbows on the table, and there was laughter in the blue eyes gazing directly into hers. 'If I

didn't know how much you disliked the man, then I would
have said you were serious.'

'I *am* serious, Gavin,' she insisted, and she hated herself
as she saw the laughter fade in his eyes. 'I know this is
sudden, and that I haven't been entirely fair to you, but
I—I've made my decision.'

'Do you mean to tell me that you've allowed me to
think that you will eventually marry me, while in fact
you've been making plans in that direction with that
Rhyno fellow?'

'Not exactly,' she shook her head as she watched his
face whiten with anger, and something more. 'Gavin, I
wouldn't have hurt you this way for anything in the world,
and whatever you may think of me, I'm really very fond
of you.'

'But you love Rhyno van der Bijl, is that it?'

His lips were drawn back in a snarl, changing his appearance to that of a stranger, and she lowered her gaze
selfconsciously, knowing that she had made of him what
he was at that moment.

'Perhaps you should take me home,' she suggested
quietly, picking up her evening purse and her wrap, but
Gavin remained seated where he was.

'Does your future husband know you're here with me
this evening?' he demanded cynically.

Kate flinched inwardly at the words 'future husband',
but she said simply, 'Yes.'

'And does he know that you've spent every evening, as
well as weekends, in my company since your father's
death?'

'Yes.'

'And he's never objected?'

Kate shook her head tiredly. 'No.'

'Well, I'm damned if I understand it,' he sighed at
length, leaning back in his chair and observing her

through narrowed eyes. 'If I were Rhyno van der Bijl then I most certainly wouldn't have allowed you to spend so much of your free time with another man.'

Kate squirmed inwardly and wished she could have told him the truth. 'Rhyno isn't the possessive type.'

'No?' Gavin laughed softly, and it was an ugly laugh that jarred her nerves. 'Then what's he doing coming towards our table and looking as if he'd like to stir up a storm?'

Her heart seemed to do a triple somersault in her breast, but before she could stir herself to glance over her shoulder she became aware of Rhyno's lean length standing beside her chair.

'It's late,' he pointed out in an abrupt, accusing voice.

'Yes, I know, but——'

'Have you told him?' Rhyno's deep voice sliced across her reply, and he jerked his thumb unceremoniously in Gavin's direction.

'Yes, I have, but I——'

'Then it's time you came home,' he interrupted her a second time, and his eyes were hard and cold as he turned towards Gavin. 'I don't want my bride looking hollow-eyed in the morning,' he explained suavely.

'Rhyno, you have——' she began furiously, but his fingers clamped about her upper arm, exerting a warning pressure as he drew her to her feet.

'You will excuse us, I'm sure,' Rhyno smiled twistedly down into Gavin's white, angry face, then he tugged at Kate's arm. 'Come along.'

Kate remained passive in his grip, embarrassingly aware of the curious glances following them as Rhyno ushered her out of the crowded restaurant, but inside she was fuming quietly like a simmering volcano which erupted the moment she was seated beside him in his white Citroën.

'May I know what that little display of possessiveness was in aid of?' she demanded icily, her hands clenching her purse tightly for fear of lashing out and striking him.

'You've been with him since seven o'clock,' he reminded her harshly as he set the car in motion and drove through the quiet streets of the town. 'It's now eleven-thirty,' he added derisively.

'So what?' she almost screamed at him in her anger.

'Four and a half hours was quite long enough for you to have told him a hundred times over that you're going to marry me.'

'It wasn't that easy,' she argued as they left the well-lit streets of Stellenbosch behind them. 'I had to wait for the right moment.'

'Since when do you care that much about anyone else's feelings, Kate?' he laughed cynically, and his laughter sliced through her painfully.

'Since when do you have the right to question me?'

'Don't put on that high-and-mighty act with me, Kate Duval,' he reprimanded her harshly, and in the dashboard light his profile was hard and unrelenting. 'You need me pretty badly at this moment, and if you don't behave yourself I might just change my mind about marrying you.'

Fear mingled with her defiance, but she was determined not to give in to it. 'In that case you'd lose La Reine, and it would serve you jolly well right!'

'I can't lose what I've never had,' he struck back at her verbally, and she flinched as the truth hit her. 'Chew on that for a while, and see if the taste appeals to you.'

A blinding fury, born of helpless frustration, gripped her. 'You imagine you hold the whip hand, don't you?'

'I don't imagine it, Kate—I know it,' he taunted her ruthlessly. 'And I shall enjoy wielding it whenever you jerk out of line in future.'

'You're a fiend!' she cried hoarsely. 'Stop this car and let me get out!'

Her hand was on the door handle, but when Rhyno ignored her and drove on she went a little crazy. She struck out at him and wrenched at the wheel, not quite knowing what she was doing at that moment, but certain only of the intense desire to get away from him.

The car lurched violently across the road and came to a screeching halt barely inches from the deep ditch on her side. The engine was switched off, but before she could leap out of the car she was taken by the shoulders and shaken so severely that it felt for a moment as if her neck would snap.

'Don't you ever do that again!' Rhyno snarled at her savagely, his face a frightening shadow inches from hers. 'You could have killed us both with your idiotic behaviour!'

'I'd rather be dead than marry someone like you!' she retorted through clenched teeth, forcing back the cry that rose to her lips when his hands tightened on her shoulders and sent stabs of pain down the length of her arms.

'You may wish yourself dead, Kate, but I would very much like to live,' his deep, harsh voice lashed her. 'I have a lot to look forward to; a woman I could love and respect one day, and children to carry on my name. Whether they grow up on La Reine, or elsewhere, makes no difference, but I won't have my dreams of the future chopped off by a worthless wildcat such as yourself who has no sense of responsibility.'

He thrust her back against the seat to start the car and, as he drove on, she could not decide which hurt most—her shoulders after the brutality she had suffered at his hands, or his wounding opinion of her character.

Whichever it was, she lapsed into a defeated silence during the rest of the short journey to Solitaire. She knew only too well that her irrational behaviour could have killed them both, and she shivered at the realisation that she had become almost a total stranger to herself.

'I suggest you go straight to bed,' Rhyno instructed coldly when they arrived at Solitaire. 'I'll be here at ten in the morning to drive you in to town, and after our marriage we have an appointment with Mr Walton.'

Kate got out of his car a little wearily, sensing that he had no intention of accompanying her to the door. He was making it embarrassingly obvious that he wanted her out of his car and out of his sight at that precise moment, and when she entered the house moments later she was surprised to discover that her eyes were stinging with unshed tears.

She slept very little that night, and when she did her dreams were confused and unhappy. She dreaded the dawn, but the hours passed relentlessly, bringing her closer to the moment when she would have to tie herself irrevocably to a man she did not love. It was all very well to think of it all as a business arrangement, but once that ring was on her finger it would give Rhyno certain rights over her, and although she had no doubt that he had no intention of ever touching her, there would always be the knowledge that he *could* if he so wished.

It was a frightening thought, and she was still trying to thrust it from her mind when the sun rose behind the Jonkershoek mountains to start its steady climb into the cloudless sky.

Aunt Edwina fussed around Kate that morning, muttering her displeasure that her niece had not taken the time to buy herself a new outfit for her wedding day, but Kate ignored her, and pulled out a cool summer suit from her wardrobe. It was the colour of unskimmed milk, and the wide collar of the jacket was trimmed with tan braid. She had worn it only once before, when she had accompanied her father to a wine-tasting luncheon at the Stellenbosch winery, and although Aunt Edwina viewed the outfit doubtfully, Kate decided that it would simply have to suffice.

'I'd better get myself ready,' Edwina sighed eventually. 'Naomi offered to come and fetch me, and she should be here shortly.'

Kate nodded soberly without speaking, but when the door closed behind her aunt she sank down on to her bed and buried her face in her hands. How, in heaven's name, was she going to live through this frightful day which was the start of an even more frightful year ahead of her? All this was because of Solitaire; she was marrying Rhyno because of Solitaire, and she had no doubt that she would still have to endure much more for this piece of land she loved so very much.

She bathed and dressed mechanically, neither knowing nor caring what she was doing. This was not how she had imagined her wedding day, and the man who would stand beside her was not the man she would have chosen voluntarily. Rhyno had spoken of one day marrying a woman he could love and respect, but she doubted very much if that cold slab he called a heart would ever melt sufficiently to know what love was.

She put an extra dab of powder on her nose and stared at herself in the mirror. Her coral-pink lipstick was the only splash of colour in her otherwise pale face, for her eyes had become dark, stormy, and dissatisfied.

There was a knock on her door and, thinking it was her aunt, she called irritably, 'Come in.'

Naomi van der Bijl entered the room, handsomely dressed in deep blue, and Kate was too surprised to rise from the dressing-table stool, but Naomi seemed not to notice her lapse as she drew up a chair and seated herself facing her.

'We have a few minutes before Rhyno arrives,' she spoke hurriedly, 'and I have something I must say to you.'

Kate stiffened, and her chin rose with a measure of defiance. 'My marriage to your son is a business arrangement, and you know that, don't you?'

'I know,' Naomi replied, a hint of sadness in her eyes.

'Then I fail to see what you could possibly have to say to me.'

'When I was a girl of twenty your father asked me to marry him,' she shocked Kate to silence. 'I was extremely fond of him, but I asked him to give me time to consider his proposal, and during that time I met my late husband. William was charming, attentive, and romantic; in fact he was all the things your father was not, and he swept me off my feet. I married him, but it was a mistake I lived to regret. Through him I lost La Reine which was my birthplace and my inheritance, and the only thing which has offered me some consolation during the past twenty years was the knowledge that La Reine was in your father's care.'

'What has this got to do with me?' Kate asked stiffly.

'You're not happy about marrying Rhyno.'

'It's a marriage I've been forced into because of my father's ridiculous will, and I shall hate every minute of this year ahead of me,' Kate admitted without hesitation or consideration for Naomi's feelings.

'It's a sacrifice you'll consider worthwhile in the end, Kate ... believe me.' Naomi leaned forward to touch Kate's hand briefly. 'You'll have Solitaire.'

'And Rhyno will eventually have La Reine,' Kate added with a touch of cynicism. 'That's really why you've come, and not because you're so concerned about me.'

'I *am* concerned about you, Kate, and I admit quite freely that I'm concerned about my son.'

'Why be concerned, Mrs van der Bijl?' Kate observed her closely. 'Through your son you'll have La Reine returned to you, and that's something worth rejoicing about, isn't it?'

Naomi's glance did not waver, but there were tears in her eyes when she shook her head and said: 'I can't rejoice about something which will cause someone else unhappiness.'

Kate felt as if she had been dealt a severe blow to her midriff, and her defiance disintegrated like mist before the sun. 'I believe you really mean that.'

A tear escaped and ran unheeded down the older woman's cheek. 'I loved La Reine as much as you love Solitaire. I know what it feels like to lose something as precious as one's inheritance, and I wouldn't want you to suffer that same fate.' She dabbed at her eyes with a lacy handkerchief, and smiled faintly. 'Consider your marriage to my son as an obstacle which must be overcome, and keep in mind that in the end Solitaire will be safe in your hands.'

'I think I know now why you came here this morning,' Kate whispered, swallowing the lump in her throat. 'You came to attach some purpose to this farcical marriage, and to help me regain my sense of direction.'

'You're very perceptive, my dear,' Naiomi smiled, but her smile made way for a frown. 'I feel that, in a way, I'm to blame for this awkward situation you find yourself in today, and I would like to make amends.'

'Why on earth should you blame yourself?' Kate demanded in surprise.

'Five years after my husband had left me, when I'd received the news of his death, your father asked me again to marry him, and I refused.'

'I didn't know that. In fact, I never even guessed that he knew you that well.'

'I'm not surprised,' Naomi smiled ruefully. 'It's not something your father would have talked about freely.'

It was strange, Kate thought, but for some reason Naomi van der Bijl's disclosure had not shocked her, and it was out of mere curiosity that she asked: 'Why did you refuse him?'

'I was afraid that some day he might think that I married him merely to save La Reine.'

'Why did you sell La Reine to him?'

Naomi sighed and lowered her gaze. 'I was in debt up to my ears, and your father made me an offer I couldn't refuse. Much as I loved La Reine, I knew that I couldn't hang on to it, and I knew that your father had always dreamed of making the two farms one.'

'Then why is he splitting them up again?' Kate frowned confusedly.

'I'm afraid I can't answer that. It's possible, I suppose, that he hoped for the opposite.'

Kate ignored the last part of her remark. 'Did my father never ask you again to marry him?'

Naomi shook her head a little sadly. 'Jacques was a proud man, and he wouldn't have risked being rejected a third time.'

'Would you have rejected him?' Kate probed curiously, and there was a flicker of sadness in Naomi's dark eyes; a sadness that caused pain.

'No, I don't think I would have.'

Kate lapsed into a contemplative silence, then she raised her troubled glance and asked hesitantly, 'Do you consider that he planned to take some kind of revenge when he drew up this complicated will?'

'I'm not sure,' Naomi replied frowningly, then she shook her head helplessly. 'I don't think anyone, except your father, knew exactly what went on in his own mind.'

A knock on Kate's bedroom door interrupted their

conversation, and Aunt Edwina entered without waiting for an invitation.

'Rhyno is here, Kate,' she announced quietly.

'Then we'd better be on our way,' Naomi remarked, rising to her feet, then she linked her arm through Aunt Edwina's and they walked out of the room, leaving Kate alone with an uncommon tightness in her chest.

She was nervous even though she told herself that she had no reason to be. She was entering into a business arrangement with Rhyno, and their marriage would be no more than a contract which would expire after twelve months. She had absolutely nothing to be nervous or jittery about, but her insides were quivering like a tightly strung bow when she walked out of her room a few minutes later to where Rhyno was waiting for her in the hall.

CHAPTER FOUR

'I SHOULD have asked before, but I'm afraid it slipped my mind,' Kate broke the strained silence in the car on the way to Stellenbosch. 'What about Barbara Owen?'

Rhyno's face remained as dark and impassive as his perfectly tailored suit and sober grey tie. 'What about her?'

'Does she know about—about us?' she asked uncomfortably, casting him a sidelong glance.

'She knows we're getting married today,' he replied bluntly.

'You told her, of course, that it was merely a business arrangement.'

His dark, angry eyes met hers briefly before he concentrated on the road once more. 'I told her nothing of the kind.'

'You mean she thinks that—that— —'

'Like Gavin Page, she thinks we've suddenly discovered that we're crazy about each other,' he finished for her with a derisive twist to his lips, and Kate shrank back against her seat when she felt her cheeks grow warm with embarrassment.

'She must have been terribly upset,' she remarked, making an effort to control her quivering nerves.

'Does it bother you?'

His words stung, insinuating that she was callous and insensitive, but she was determined not to let him guess that it had hurt as she said coldly, 'Not if it doesn't bother you.'

They lapsed into a silence which lasted until they

arrived at the magistrate's offices where Aunt Edwina and Naomi van der Bijl awaited them, and Kate's legs were shaking beneath her when they entered the building.

The ceremony was impersonal and businesslike, and the magistrate's voice was cold and emotionless as he went through the brief ritual of joining two people together in the eyes of the law, but Kate's hand trembled when Rhyno slipped that plain gold band on to her finger. It was a perfect fit, but her mind was too numb to register anything beyond that. She signed her name as Katherine Duval for the last time, and a few minutes later they walked out into the sunshine again. She was aware of Aunt Edwina and Naomi kissing her cheek, and then she was seated beside Rhyno in his Citroën and being driven to Hubert Walton's office.

Hubert could not see them at once, and while they waited Kate somehow managed to gather her scattered wits about her. Rhyno sat beside her, his arms crossed over his broad chest, and his eyes fixed broodingly on the autumn leaf pattern of the carpet beneath their feet. What was he thinking? Did he feel as detached from everything as she did? In the breast pocket of his jacket was a document which proved beyond doubt that she was his wife, but he was, in actual fact, as much a free agent as he had been before, and down in the very depths of her being she was still Kate Duval.

He looked up suddenly and their eyes met and held for frightening seconds before he remarked cynically, 'Did you expect to feel different?'

His uncanny habit of reading her thoughts was nothing new to her, but it had never unnerved her more than at that moment. She tried to think of something to say, but couldn't, and then Hubert's secretary was announcing that the attorney was awaiting them in his office.

Hubert Walton observed them in silence when they

entered the room and seated themselves on the opposite side of his desk. The grey eyes beneath the bushy brows were cool and expressionless at first, then a flicker of humour lit up their depths.

'It's a damnable situation,' he began at length. 'I'm not quite certain, under the circumstances, whether I should offer you my congratulations or my condolences.'

'Neither,' Rhyno's deep voice announced abruptly before Kate could open her mouth to speak. 'Let's just get down to the core of the matter in question, and get it over with as quickly as possible.'

'Yes, well . . .' Hubert cleared his throat and lowered his glance to the papers on the desk before him. 'There's very little left for me to tell you, but it's nevertheless important.'

'We gathered that, and that's why we're here,' Kate said quickly before Rhyno had a second opportunity to snap at the attorney, and without wasting further time Hubert Walton briefly outlined their future.

'It's expected of you, Rhyno, to move into Solitaire with Kate. You will both receive an adequate monthly allowance for the next twelve months, and all expenses and profits with regard to the estate will be dealt with through my office.' He looked up and glanced from one to the other. 'Are there any questions?'

'Just one,' Rhyno said abruptly. 'What happens in a year from now?'

'I shall approach you with one final question before Jacques Duval's file is closed.'

'I know what that question will be, and I can give you the answer right now,' Kate bit out the words, the very essence of her resentment returning to spark the blue flames of anger in her eyes. 'No, we do not wish to continue with our marriage,' she stated coldly.

'Don't be hasty, Kate,' Hubert warned. 'You may both feel differently in a year from now.'

'Don't bet on it, Mr Walton,' Rhyno intervened harshly, and the attorney ceased to exist momentarily as Kate's angry glance clashed with Rhyno's in a silent battle that left neither of them the victor.

Hubert Walton coughed politely, drawing attention to himself in that manner, and when Kate and Rhyno turned to face him, he said somewhat drily, 'Well, that's all I have to say to you at the moment, except to wish you both the very best in this venture.'

They drove back to Solitaire in silence; two strangers with nothing to say to each other, and nothing in common except an inheritance which resulted in the unfamiliar weight of that gold band on Kate's finger. She felt like wrenching it off and flinging it out of the window, but that would achieve nothing. They were legally married, and it made no difference at all whether she was wearing a ring or not.

Naomi van der Bijl and Aunt Edwina awaited them at Solitaire, and Rhyno opened a bottle of the estate's sparkling white wine before they sat down to lunch. The conversation simply would not flow, and the silences became progressively longer. Kate's plate was returned to the kitchen almost untouched, and when they had had their tea Naomi announced that it was time she went home. Rhyno got up to accompany his mother out to her car, but Kate remained seated, facing her aunt broodingly. Close to Kate's hand, on the white damask tablecloth, stood the glass of wine she had been loathe to drink. It had lost its sparkle, and had gone as flat as she felt at that moment.

When Rhyno entered the dining hall a few minutes later, Kate rose to her feet and excused herself. 'I'm going to my room.'

'Kate!' Aunt Edwina's voice stopped her before she had

reached the door. 'I've had your things moved into the master bedroom.'

The fire of anger was in her eyes, but in her chest she felt positively claustrophobic. 'Who gave you permission to do that without consulting me?'

'There wasn't much time to consult you in this matter, but you surely realise that although *we* know the true reason for this marriage, it's preferable that the servants remain in ignorance.'

'Your aunt is right, Kate,' Rhyno intervened, and she cast him a swift, chilling glance.

'Kindly stay out of this!'

His mouth tightened and his thin nostrils flared. 'This affects me as much as it affects you, and if you're too stubborn to recognise the wisdom of your aunt's actions, then be it on your own head if the estate workers begin to speculate about us.'

'They can speculate all they like!'

'And in the process they'll lose their respect for you.'

The arrow found its mark with familiar precision, leaving her with the sickening thought that she was as transparent as glass to this man she had married that morning. Somehow he was familiar with her weaknesses, and he used his knowledge like a weapon.

'You think you have all the answers, don't you?' she muttered in a voice that shook with suppressed anger as she stared up into his expressionless face.

'Kate . . .' Aunt Edwina intervened gently, but Kate whirled on her in the aftermath of her fury.

'Oh, leave me alone, both of you!' she cried in a choked voice, then she ran out of the house, neither knowing, nor caring where she went, just as long as she could rid herself of that awful feeling that she had been caught in a trap from which there was no escape.

She paused for breath under the oak tree at the end of

the drive, then she walked on through the vineyards, the heels of her expensive shoes digging into the soft earth. The sun came out from behind a stray cloud to sting her face and arms, but it did not trouble her, and she walked on through the vineyard until she reached the clearing ahead of her. To her right stood a gnarled old acacia tree, and she wandered towards it to seek shelter beneath its thorny branches. She stood there for a moment, drinking in the blessed peace of her surroundings while her gaze dwelt on the mountains in the distance with their rocky peaks jutting into the sky, then she walked on until she reached the small stone hut where she had played as a child, and an audible sigh escaped her.

Oh, those carefree days when her only problem had been slipping into the house without Aunt Edwina noticing the mud she had messed on her clothes, or the tear in her new frock. Those problems had not been insurmountable. There had always been someone at home to wash away or patch up the evidence of her misdemeanours, but nothing could wash away or patch up the mess she was in at that moment. She was trapped by that circle of gold on her finger, and what hurt most was the knowledge that her father was the cause of it all.

She sat down on the upright tree stump which had been partially hollowed out to serve as an imaginary oven for the many mud pies she had baked as a child, and helpless tears filled her eyes and paved their way down her cheeks. She despised herself for being so weak, but she could not stop the tears once they had started, and she cried silently for long minutes before she managed to control herself to a certain degree. She longed for those days when Aunt Edwina's shoulder had offered her the comfort she had needed, but those days were gone for ever. Aunt Edwina was against her just like everyone else, she thought bitterly, but then she realised that she was allowing herself

to become submerged in a well of self-pity, and she pulled
herself together sharply while she used the back of her
hand to dash away the evidence of her recent tears.

Her action made the sun glint on the ring Rhyno had
placed on her finger that morning, and she stared down
at it fixedly. Her hand had almost disappeared in his big,
rough palm when he had slipped the ring on to her finger,
and she recalled now how she had looked up to find him
observing her with a look in his dark eyes which had
momentarily stilled the breath in her throat. It had been
an odd, penetrating look which had left her shaken and
disturbed for a time, but she thrust the memory from her
almost as if it were something distasteful.

Kate could not say for sure how long she sat there, but
she was jerked out of her thoughts when Rhyno's white,
dusty Citroën came to a crunching halt a little distance
from her. He had changed into beige slacks and a green
open-necked shirt, she noticed vaguely when he climbed
out of the car, but when he approached her with that
lithe, panther-like tread she was all at once made incredibly aware of the virile masculinity encased in that
lean, hard body. The desire to run, and never stop running, swept through her with an equal suddenness, and it
was only with the greatest effort that she managed to
remain seated on that tree stump with her eyes riveted to
his approaching figure.

'You're a long way from home,' he remarked casually
when he stood directly in front of her with his feet planted
firmly apart, and his thumbs hooked into the narrow
leather belt hugging his hips.

'So what!' she snapped defiantly.

'Don't blame your aunt for doing what she thought
was best, Kate.'

'Best for whom, may I ask?'

'For all of us.'

Kate looked away from him to where a patch of wispy clouds shifted lazily across the sky, and her mouth tightened stubbornly. 'I refuse to share the master bedroom with you, and if you and my aunt think I'll carry this pretence that far, then you can both think again!'

'There's a perfectly comfortable bed in the dressing-room, and someone very kindly put fresh linen on it.'

He was laughing at her, she could see it in his eyes, and helpless anger loaded her voice heavily with sarcasm. 'How nice!'

'What are you afraid of, Kate?' he asked with a derisive twist to his mouth. 'Are you afraid I might at some time become feverish with desire for you, and demand my conjugal rights?'

'Don't be ridiculous!' she snapped, her cheeks flaming.

'You're the one who's being ridiculous.'

'Oh, go away, and leave me alone!' she shouted angrily, jumping up and walking swiftly away from him.

'I'm damned if I will!' He was beside her in an instant, his hands biting into her shoulders as he turned her roughly to face him. 'Stop behaving like a child, Kate, and accept the fact that we're going to have to live this way for the next year. We entered into a business agreement, remember, so stop this nonsense and honour your commitments like the sensible adult you're supposed to be.'

'Stop preaching to me, Rhyno van der Bijl!' she snapped, her eyes blazing up into his as she tried to free herself.

'Kate——'

'And take your hands off me!'

He released her so abruptly that she staggered, but his face was taut with anger, and had she not been so stubborn she would have adhered to the warning signals flashing through her mind when he said quietly, 'Get into the car. Your aunt is waiting for us to join her for tea.'

Kate brushed a long, silvery strand of hair out of her eyes, and glanced up at him defiantly. 'I'll walk, thank you.'

'If you're going to behave like a child, then I'm going to have to treat you like one,' he announced savagely, and before she had time to guess his intention he was swinging her off her feet and carrying her towards his car.

'Let me go, you beast!' she cried, beating him about the chest and shoulders with her clenched fists, but he merely laughed infuriatingly and tightened his arms about her.

When he reached the car he set her on her feet to open the door on the passenger side, but his arm remained about her waist like a vice despite her efforts to twist herself free. She was thrust unceremoniously into the front seat, and the door was slammed in her face, shutting off her angry protests.

Kate was not beaten yet, and when Rhyno walked round the front of the car towards the driver's side, she wrenched open the door and almost fell out in her haste to get away from him, and the peculiar feelings he had aroused when he had held her in his arms. She had been a good sprinter at school, but that was some years ago, and then, she had to admit, she had never tried it before in high-heeled shoes. Rhyno caught up with her before she had gone very far, and this time his hands were punishing as he literally dragged her back to the car while she fought like a wildcat and subjected him to a barrage of insults.

Without a word, he flung her face down across the bonnet of the car and twisted her arms behind her back in a way that made her fear they would be torn out of her shoulder sockets. He held her arms there with his one hand, while with the other he pulled off his belt, and then, to her horror, he was tying her hands securely behind her back.

Tears stung her eyes, but she blinked them back rapidly as she twisted her head to glance at him over her shoulder. 'You're a brute, and I *hate* you!' she cried in a choked voice.

'You may hate me as much as you please, but I'm taking you home, and you're going to apologise to your aunt for speaking to her in that insubordinate manner after lunch.'

'I'll do nothing of the kind!' she spat out the words vehemently.

'We'll see about that,' he replied harshly, giving the belt about her wrists a final vicious tug that made her bite down hard on her lip in an effort not to cry out in pain, then she was thrust into the car and the door was slammed on her a second time.

Stripped of her dignity, she had only her fury left, and it shook through her with a force that made her feel murderous at that moment when Rhyno slid behind the wheel and turned the key in the ignition.

'You can't treat me like this and think you can get away with it!' she informed him through tightly clenched teeth, but his face remained a bronze mask of unconcern as he glanced at her briefly.

'You asked for it, Kate.'

'I'll make you pay for this if it's the last thing I do!' she hissed, blinking back her tears of anger, and twisting her hands behind her back in an effort to release them, but Rhyno had tied her wrists so securely that every movement inflicted pain.

She sat there in an ungainly, huddled heap, glaring at him in silence while he took her back to the house, but it was she who broke the silence when he parked the Citroën in the circular drive and walked round to open the door for her.

'Untie my hands,' she said over her shoulder.

'Are you going to do as you're told?'

'Go to the devil!' she cried furiously.

'Very well, then.'

'*No!*' she exclaimed anxiously when he took her by the arms, intending to lift her out of the car.

'Have you changed your mind?'

His eyes challenged her, and she hated him more than ever at that moment as she said icily, 'You're a bastard, Rhyno, and I'll get you for this.'

'That's not the attitude to adopt if you don't want me to drag you into the house like a naughty child,' he mocked her, and his hands tightened threateningly on her arms.

'Do that, Rhyno, and I shall never forgive you.'

'That doesn't scare me, Kate,' he laughed harshly, 'but if you give me your word that you will behave, and do as you're told, then I'll untie you.'

The embarrassment of being taken into the house while bound like some sort of criminal was too much even for Kate, and she submitted to his will, albeit reluctantly. 'You have my word.'

Her hands were untied, and she sat for a moment rubbing her wrists gently where the leather had bitten into the tender flesh, then a large, rough hand gripped her arm above the elbow, and she was practically lifted out of the front seat. She might have appeared outwardly docile as he escorted her into the house, but inwardly she was fuming and, when they joined Aunt Edwina in the living-room, Kate rattled off the appropriate apology.

If her aunt was surprised, then she gave no sign, but Kate had never felt more like doing someone a physical injury than at that moment when she glimpsed that look of triumph on Rhyno's lean face. *Oh, how she hated this man!*

She did not join in the conversation while they had tea, and she left soon after Rhyno excused himself to check on the fermentation tanks in the cellars. She had seen Aunt Edwina's glance stray towards the marks which were still visible on her wrists, and she was in no mood to explain how they had got there.

The need for a change of clothing forced her in the direction of the master bedroom, and when she closed the door behind her she leaned against it and stared about the spacious, airy room for several seconds. It had been used for guests over the years, and Kate had been too young to remember the time when her father had shared this room with her mother.

She stared at the large four-poster bed with its heavy crimson drapes to match the curtains at the window, and felt a little sick inside. She had dreamed of sharing this room, and that enormous bed, with the man she loved, but instead she would be spending the next year occupying it alone. She could not blame fate entirely, it had been helped along magnanimously by her father, and here she was, married to a man like Rhyno van der Bijl, and knowing that she was going to hate every minute of it.

She wandered into the dressing-room where, as Rhyno had said, someone had put fresh linen on the single bed in the corner. She stood there a little hesitantly, glancing towards the right, then sighed with relief. She had forgotten that there was a door leading off the dressing-room into the passage, which meant that Rhyno did not necessarily have to make a thoroughfare of her room, and with a bathroom just across the passage he would have as much privacy as she would have. The only problem was her clothes, but that, too, had been taken care of. The cupboards in the dressing-room contained only Rhyno's clothes, and she cast a cynical glance over his sober suits in various shades of grey and brown. On the dresser, with the small mirror above it, lay his hairbrushes, and a few personal belongings, but otherwise the room looked singularly bare of any personal touch which could have given her a further insight into the character of the man who had leapt, in the space of a few short weeks, from estate manager to her husband.

Husband. She shrank inwardly from the word with a measure of distaste. She could never think of Rhyno in that respect. He was merely the man she had married to comply with the conditions in her father's will.

She walked back into the bedroom and opened the large wardrobe against the wall facing the window. Her clothes were all there, neatly folded in the shelves, or hanging on the hangers, and when she glanced over her shoulder she could see that her personal toiletries had been set out neatly on the dressing-table. She washed and changed quickly into a colourful skirt and crisp white blouse, but when she touched up her make-up and brushed her hair, she stared at herself in the mirror for long seconds. She had tied her hair away from her face with a blue silk scarf, and it made her look younger, almost vulnerable, but this was not what she was thinking of at that moment. She was thinking of that brief and binding ceremony which had taken place that morning, and if it were not for that gold band on her finger she could almost believe that it had never happened. But it *had*, and for the next year she would carry the hateful title of *Mrs Rhyno van der Bijl*.

She had a peculiar feeling that she was being suffocated and, flinging her brush on to the dressing-table, she stormed out of the room, and out of the house in search of air.

That evening, when they sat down to dinner, Kate and Rhyno faced each other from the extremities of the table with Aunt Edwina seated somewhere in between. Kate was about to open her mouth to demand who gave Rhyno the right to sit in her father's chair when Aunt Edwina forestalled her with, 'I hope you don't mind my putting you in Jacques' place, Rhyno, but it's nice to have a man at the head of the table again.'

Kate's mouth snapped shut into a tight, angry line as Rhyno smiled faintly and murmured something she could not quite catch, then the moment passed as the first course was served.

'It's nice to have a man at the head of the table again,' Aunt Edwina's remark echoed repeatedly through Kate's mind during dinner, and she thought cynically, 'Well, let him bask in this unexpected glory. When this year has passed I shall personally hoist him out of his now exalted position!'

Their coffee was served to them in the living-room and, when Kate had placed her empty cup in the tray, she excused herself and went for a walk. She was too incredibly tense to think of going to bed, and too annoyed that her aunt had accepted everything so calmly.

A cool south-easterly breeze was pushing up from the coast between the Helderberg and Jonkershoek mountains, and the nip in the air was just sufficient to remind her that the summer was at an end. The harvest would go on for at least another two weeks, and soon the new young wines would have to be tested and nurtured with loving care along the way to becoming one of the superb, full-bodied wines Solitaire was known for.

Kate sat down on the bench beneath the shadows of the old oak, and sighed heavily. She would have given anything to be in Cape Town with Gavin at that moment. They would have laughed about silly little things, and they would have had fun, but instead she sat there alone in the darkness with no one to talk to, and no one who would understand.

A movement caught her eye, and she glanced towards the house just in time to see Rhyno walking briskly towards the estate truck. He was going to check on the fermentation tanks, and she supposed she ought to be grateful that she had someone on Solitaire who was as keen and conscientious about the winemaking process as Rhyno was, but the thought offered her no comfort at all.

Later that evening, when she sat in front of the dressing-table going through the nightly ritual of brushing her hair before going to bed, she heard Rhyno's footsteps in the passage. She stiffened automatically and, lowering her brush on to the dressing-table, her hands moved of their own volition to tighten the belt of her silk dressing-gown. Her heart gave a sickening jolt when she heard him pause briefly outside her door, then he walked on and went into the dressing-room.

For some inexplicable reason she sat there rigidly while she listened to him move about. She heard the dressing-room door open and close, then she heard him in the shower across the passage. She relaxed momentarily, and picked up her brush to continue brushing her hair until it shone like pure silver, but a certain degree of tension remained with her, and she finally got to her feet to pace the floor restlessly. She heard Rhyno return to the dressing-room, she heard him moving about, opening and closing cupboard doors, and it felt strange to think that only a wooden door separated her from the man she had married that morning; a man who meant nothing and never could mean anything to her.

A sharp knock on the dressing-room door jarred every nerve in her body, and her voice betrayed some of her tension when she demanded sharply. 'What do you want?'

'I have something here for you,' Rhyno replied, his

voice muffled through the door, and she was instantly on her guard.

'What is it?'

'It's something that should make you sleep easier,' he replied, and the word 'tranquilliser' leapt into her mind.

'I shall sleep perfectly well without——' The door opened abruptly, and the rest of her sentence seemed to die a natural death in her throat when she found herself staring at Rhyno in his black towelling robe with the belt tied carelessly about his waist, and his hair still damp from his shower. Her eyes became riveted to the spot where his robe parted to reveal his tanned, hair-roughened chest, and for one wild moment resentment flared within her. No man had the right to look so vital, so virile, and so destructively masculine, she thought frantically as her senses responded with a will of their own, but when her heart joined in with a heavy thudding against her ribs she forced herself to meet those dark, bold eyes. 'Who gave you permission to come in here?' she demanded haughtily.

'Carrying on a conversation through a closed door is quite unsatisfactory, don't you agree?' he smiled faintly, thrusting his hands into the pockets of his robe and advancing towards her.

'Say what you have to say, and get out.'

He paused beside the dressing-table, and raised one sardonic eyebrow, then those bold, intensely probing eyes shifted slowly down the length of her, lingering on the curves of her slender body beneath her silk dressing-gown, and igniting twin spots of colour in her cheeks which deepened when his eyes met hers again.

'Like your namesake in Shakespeare's play, you're really quite a shrew, and if my interests were not elsewhere I might have found it enjoyable taming you, Kate.'

There was a nervous fluttering in her stomach, but her

eyes sparkled with mockery. 'You fancy yourself as Petruchio, then?'

His mouth twitched, but his expression remained stern as he said harshly, 'There's no doubt in my mind that a few hard slaps on your posterior from time to time would put a more civil tongue in your head.'

'And I have no doubt that you're the most arrogant, insufferable and self-opinionated creature God ever made, and I *hate* you!' she hissed at him.

'Someone who hates as well as you do, Kate, will love with an equal passion.' His eyes flicked over her with a dangerously sensuous fire in their depths, and they lingered on that tell-tale pulse at the base of her throat which was beating frantically with an emotion she could not grasp. 'Intriguing thought, isn't it?' he added softly, as if he was aware of her confusion.

'What a pity you'll never know whether your assumption is correct,' she replied daringly, but she knew the instant she had spoken that it had been a mistake, for his eyes narrowed as he approached her with that slow stealthiness of a jungle cat.

'Is that a challenge, Kate?'

She backed away from him until she stood framed against the crimson curtains, and her hands moved involuntarily to the belt of her dressing-gown. 'It was a statement of fact, that's all, and if you come any closer I'll scream!'

He smiled that twisted, cynical smile as he paused no more than a pace away from her. 'Are you afraid I might discover I'm right?'

'I'm not afraid of anything,' she protested defiantly, the scent of his particular brand of shaving cream filling her nostrils and stirring her bewildered senses, and she lashed out at him in resentment. 'All I've ever felt for you is revulsion.'

During the brief ensuing silence the air between them seemed to be charged with electricity, then Rhyno's face darkened with a frightening anger, and his lips drew back from his strong, white teeth in something close to a snarl as he said thickly, 'My God, you asked for this, Kate!'

She should have anticipated his actions, but she didn't, and the next instant she found herself locked in a fierce embrace that pinned her arms helplessly at her sides. His thighs were pressed against hers, and her breasts were crushed against the hard wall of his chest, but nothing was worse than that cruel, punishing mouth against her own which forced her head back until it felt as though her neck would snap. She was too stunned at first to react, but when she finally struggled against those imprisoning arms her efforts merely made her more aware of the male hardness of his body against her soft, feminine curves, and every nerve and pulse began to throb with a strange rhythm that sent an incredible weakness surging into her limbs. He forced her lips apart with his own, and his intimate invasion of her mouth sent a shock of unfamiliar sensations rippling through her. She should have felt insulted, but instead she found herself responding until she felt drugged and no longer capable of coherent thought.

Rhyno released her abruptly, and she staggered away from him, clutching at the curtains behind her for support. She felt dazed, and more than just slightly bewildered, and she had a horrible feeling that it showed on her face while Rhyno's features remained composed and shuttered. He seemed to display none of the symptoms she was experiencing at that moment, no shortness of breath, nor frantically throbbing pulses, and although she hated him for it, she could not help envying him his calm, unruffled appearance while she stood there feeling shattered to the very core of her being.

'I believe this key locks the dressing-room door,' his harsh voice grated along her sensitive nerves, and he flipped a metal object on to the dressing-table. 'Lock the door, if you like, but you need have no fear that I shall force my attentions on someone who's done nothing but arouse my contempt!'

Kate stood as if turned to stone until he had disappeared into the dressing-room and closed the door firmly behind him. Only then did she move gropingly towards the bed to sink weakly into its springy softness. Nothing like this had ever happened to her before, and something warned her that if she wanted to emerge from this business arrangement unscathed, then she would have to take care that it never happened again.

CHAPTER FIVE

KATE's fingers curled about the key. It was cold and hard against her palm, as cold and hard as Rhyno's face had been the night before when he had told her that she had aroused nothing but his contempt. She had been too distraught afterwards to think of locking the door into the dressing-room, but it had, after all, not been necessary. They had both said enough to erect a barrier between them which was as solid as an impenetrable steel wall, and she knew that it would take more than an ordinary key to unlock the metaphorical doors they had slammed in each other's faces.

She dropped the key into the dressing-table drawer and pushed it shut with a grimace. She had had difficulty in falling asleep last night. She had been too shattered by Rhyno's kisses, and too bewildered by her own feelings. She had imagined she would hate him more than ever this morning, but instead she felt only remorse, and something else she could not quite define.

It was going to be a grim Sunday, she decided when she left her room to join Rhyno and Aunt Edwina for breakfast, but she had no idea just how grim the next few weeks were going to be.

During the remainder of the harvest Kate and Rhyno worked together as a team even though they spoke to each other only when it was absolutely necessary, and they both seemed equally incapable of doing anything to eliminate the icy atmosphere which reigned supreme whenever they were together. Kate decided that it was best to leave things as they were, but Aunt Edwina apparently had other ideas.

Late one evening, when the harvest was at an end and the winemaking had begun in earnest, Aunt Edwina confronted Kate in the living-room before she could retire for the night.

'There's been a distinct chill in this house since your marriage to Rhyno,' Edwina started her obvious campaign to end the cold war. 'There was a time when the two of you used to speak to each other, even if it was only in an argumentative way, but these days there are those long-drawn-out silences, and I'm getting rather tired of hearing my own voice.'

'I'm sorry, Aunt Edwina,' Kate murmured, lowering her gaze and feeling guilty that her aunt should suffer because of the awkward situation between Rhyno and herself.

'Being sorry is all very well, Kate,' Aunt Edwina continued determinedly, 'but something will have to be done about the situation. It can't go on like this indefinitely, and if you don't want the months ahead to become unbearable for everyone concerned, then the two of you will have to do something about it.'

Kate sighed and seated herself on the arm of her aunt's chair. 'We said some terrible things to each other the day we were married.'

'Then I suggest you put it right.'

'It isn't as easy as that.'

'Nothing important is ever easy.'

'But why should I be the one to do something about it?' Kate demanded indignantly.

'Knowing you, Kate, you most probably needed very little encouragement to make use of that barbed tongue of yours,' her aunt replied drily.

Kate looked at the woman who had been both mother and aunt to her since her second birthday, and an affec-

tionate smile lifted the corners of her mouth. 'I suppose
you're right, Aunt Edwina.'

'Then do something about it,' her aunt persisted, and
when Kate did not reply she added anxiously, 'You surely
don't want the situation to continue the way it is, do
you?'

Kate stared down at the carpet with a mixture of indecision and wariness. She was not quite sure what she
wanted, but anything would be preferable to the existing
cold war between Rhyno and herself.

'Where's Rhyno?' she asked absently, still not sure what
she was going to do.

'He mentioned something about the wine in the ferm-
intation tanks reaching the critical stage, and my guess is
that you'll find him in the cellars doing a four-hourly
check.' Aunt Edwina placed an encouraging hand on
Kate's arm. 'He's been there since after dinner this evening, and I doubt if he'll come at all tonight, so why not
take him a flask of coffee?'

Kate hesitated momentarily, then she dropped a light
kiss on her aunt's forehead and rose to her feet. 'I'll do as
you suggest, but if I come away with insults ringing in my
ears, then don't expect me to repeat the performance!'

Twenty minutes later she was parking the small jeep
outside the building which housed the large wooden vats
and steel fermentation tanks. The light was on in the small
room used as an office, and taking the basket off the seat
beside her, she climbed out of the jeep and entered the
cellar quietly.

The door to the office stood slightly ajar, and she
walked in without knocking to find Rhyno seated behind
the desk with one of his favourite pipes clenched between
his teeth. He looked up suddenly from the papers he had
been studying, and she felt decidedly uncomfortable when
his cool, enquiring gaze flicked over her, taking in her

faded denims and pink and white striped blouse.

He took his pipe out of his mouth and wiped the corner of his lips with the back of his hand. 'Why aren't you at home and in bed?'

His voice was terse and unfriendly, but she ignored it determinedly as she placed the basket on the desk. 'I thought you might want a cup of coffee and a little help.'

'That's generous of you.'

Was that sarcasm she heard in his voice, or merely surprise? she wondered as she unscrewed the flask's cap and poured coffee into the mugs. She felt nervous and ill at ease, and not quite sure that she was doing the right thing, but when she handed him his coffee his tired face struck a sensitive chord.

'Why don't you go home and get some rest?' she suggested tentatively. 'I'll stay here for a while.'

He leaned back in his chair with the mug between his hands, and shook his head. 'I can't leave you here alone, Kate.'

The ice was miraculously broken, and they were back on the old footing. She knew it when anger and resentment rose within her like a tidal wave. 'I've gone through this ritual for quite a number of years now, and my father never once doubted my capabilities.'

'Sheathe your claws, Kate,' he ordered harshly. 'I was referring to you as a woman, and your safety if you should remain here alone.'

Her anger subsided as swiftly as it had risen, and her eyes were laughing at him now. 'Do you imagine someone might be hiding behind the vats to pounce on me?'

'You never know.'

'Don't be silly,' she argued. 'The workers are a superstitious lot, and very few of them would risk coming here at night.'

'What makes you say that?'

'They believe the underground cellars are haunted.' She seated herself on the corner of the desk, and when he didn't reply she glanced at him curiously. 'Didn't you know?'

'That's ridiculous,' he said abruptly, thrusting his pipe into his mouth and lighting it. 'This building was erected in your father's time.'

'This section, yes,' she nodded, 'but the section where the vats are situated is over two hundred years old, and the workers firmly believe that any building that old *must* have a ghost.'

'All the more reason, then, why I can't leave you here on your own,' he mocked her.

'I don't believe in ghosts,' she retorted abruptly, raising her mug to her lips and sipping at the hot coffee.

'Perhaps not, but I have a better solution,' Rhyno announced. 'Why don't you stay and keep me company? I've a long night ahead of me, and the hours drag when one is on one's own.' A cloud of smoke drifted towards the high ceiling, and the pleasant aroma of his pipe tobacco hovered about her. 'What about it, Kate?'

Her eyes met his and she wondered if he knew why she had joined him there in the cellars, but she thrust this uncomfortable thought from her and said soberly, 'I'll stay, if you like.'

They sat there in silence for some minutes, then he placed his empty mug on the desk blotter. 'You make a good cup of coffee.'

'Thanks,' she said without looking at him.

'We don't have much to say to each other, do we?'

'No,' she sighed, putting her own mug aside, and turning her head to look at him just in time to see a faint smile curving his mouth, but it disappeared so swiftly that she could almost have imagined it.

'If you're going to keep me company all night, then we

shall have to think of something,' Rhyno announced drily, and she grasped at the first thing that came to mind.

'Tell me about yourself,' she said. 'Why did you go to school in Cape Town instead of here in Stellenbosch?'

His mouth twitched, but his eyes remained expressionless. 'Who told you that?'

'My father,' she replied, not particularly interested in the topic of conversation she had chosen.

'I started off my education here in Stellenbosch, but when my mother sold La Reine to your father I was sent to a school in Cape Town,' he explained tolerantly. 'Someone who obviously thought a great deal of my mother paid for my education right through to university, and it was this person's wish that I attend a private school in Cape Town.'

Kate's interest quickened, and she thought at once of her father. He had had a very high opinion of Naomi van der Bijl, but whether he would have taken a hand in the education of her son was something she could not be certain of, and she cast the thought aside, labelling it ridiculous.

'Do you know who this person is?' she asked cautiously.

'No.'

'Have you never tried to find out?'

'I've tried, but without much success,' he replied, placing his pipe in the ashtray and leaning back in his chair with his hands clasped behind his dark head.

His action made his shirt pull tightly across his muscled chest, and she looked away, remembering only too vividly the feel of its hardness against her soft breasts.

Directing her thoughts rather frantically in a different direction, she asked, 'What made you study viticulture?'

'An interest in winemaking, naturally, and the vague hope that I might one day be able to work on a farm such as La Reine.'

'So when my father advertised for an estate manager you jumped at the opportunity.'

'Not quite,' his abrupt reply doused that flicker of cynicism within her. 'I had a good job with a reasonably bright future ahead of me, whereas here I had no future, only the pleasure of working on the farm I'd loved so much as a child.'

'What made you decide eventually to take the job?'

His hard mouth twisted into a semblance of a smile, as if her question amused and angered him simultaneously. 'I applied for the job, and when your father asked me to come for an interview I was impressed by his knowledge.'

'And seeing La Reine again naturally influenced your decision,' she added without rancour this time.

There was a prolonged silence, then Rhyno sat forward in his chair with his arms resting on the desk so that his hands almost touched her thigh. 'You still resent me, don't you.'

It was a statement, not a question, and it shook her considerably. She knew he was watching her intently, but she could not meet his eyes, and her hands tightened on the edge of the desk as she paused to analyse her feelings.

'I don't resent you so much at the moment,' she replied quietly and truthfully. 'I'm well aware of the fact that I need your help now that my father is no longer here, but I do resent having to marry you to eventually gain my rightful inheritance.'

'When you speak of your rightful inheritance, do you feel you've been cheated out of La Reine?'

'No, I don't.' Her eyes widened, and when they met his they were filled with unmistakable sincerity. 'My father always said that La Reine would never be mine, and I accepted that. La Reine's wines are processed here on Solitaire, but that's all there is to it.'

Rhyno frowned, and his dark brows almost met to form a sombre line. 'Do you think your father had intentions of selling La Reine at some time or another?'

'Perhaps,' she gestured helplessly with her hands, 'but he changed his mind, of course, when you came along.'

He nodded abruptly, and his eyes mocked her as he referred to himself as 'The villain of the piece'.

Kate sustained his glance for a moment, not denying, nor agreeing with his remark, but his mood changed abruptly, and when his penetrating gaze aroused that odd fluttering in her breast she slid off the desk and asked abruptly, 'When do you have to check the tanks?'

'Right now,' he said, glancing at his wrist watch. 'Want to come along?'

'Just try and stop me,' she announced, and they left the office together to test and taste the young wines during this critical period in the fermentation tanks.

Kate spent the night in the cellars with Rhyno. In between the four-hourly checks they discussed winemaking techniques, drank coffee, and eventually took turns to sleep for a few hours on the comfortable camp bed in the corner of the office. When morning came they were both a little hollow-eyed and tired, but the reward they would eventually receive would be worth it all.

They had shared a common interest that night, but somehow it had brought them no closer together than they had been before, and their relationship drifted back to what it had been before their marriage.

'At least you're speaking to each other again,' Aunt Edwina remarked one morning when Kate had tea with her out on the terrace. 'I couldn't have taken those chilly silences a day longer.'

Kate felt amused, but she said nothing. Aunt Edwina would never understand the turmoil going on inside her; how could she, when Kate could not even understand it herself at times?

*

Kate had been married more than a month when she met Gavin in town one afternoon while she was wading through her shopping list. She had not seen him since that night when Rhyno had literally dragged her from his presence in the restaurant and, quite frankly, she had never dreamed that he would still want to have anything to do with her after the way she had treated him.

She felt a little awkward when she found herself face to face with him in the street, but his blue eyes laughed at her in that familiar way, and she found herself relaxing.

'Is there time for you to have tea with me somewhere?' he asked.

'Of course there is,' she said at once.

Gavin ordered tea in the tea-room across the street, and when it was brought to their table Kate poured.

'I haven't seen you in weeks,' he said when she passed him his cup.

'We've been rather busy out at Solitaire,' she replied vaguely, stirring her own tea and taking a sip.

'Kate . . .' his gaze travelled to the wedding ring on her finger, 'I'm afraid I didn't take the news of your marriage very well, but we can still be friends, can't we?'

'I'd like that, Gavin,' she smiled, wondering if he cared enough to wait, but she shelved the thought hastily.

'Are you happy, Kate? he questioned unexpectedly, and her eyes widened in surprise.

'Why do you ask?'

'Just curious,' he shrugged, and when she made no attempt to answer him, he repeated his question a little more urgently. 'Are you happy?'

'I'm as happy as anyone could hope to be, I suppose,' she replied with extreme caution.

His eyes met hers intently across the rim of his cup. 'Your marriage isn't a success, then?'

'I never said that,' she argued hastily, but Gavin merely smiled with something close to satisfaction.

'You can't fool me, Kate.'

'Gavin, you're mistaken, I——'

'All right, I won't persist in that direction,' he hastily interrupted her protest, 'but I want you to know that I'll be hanging around just in case, and all you have to do is call.'

She stared at him contemplatively for a moment, then she smiled mischievously. 'You say that almost as if you hope my marriage is going to fail!'

'Not quite,' he grinned back at her, 'but if it does, then I'll be there to pick up the pieces.'

'How melodramatic!' Kate laughed, and that unfamiliar tension eased slightly between them.

'When do I see you again?' Gavin demanded at length, his blue gaze capturing hers.

'What about coming out to Solitaire for dinner on Friday evening?' she suggested after only a brief hesitation.

'I thought you were never going to ask,' he grinned.

'See you at six-thirty on Friday, then,' she said, gathering up her parcels and getting to her feet. 'And thanks for the tea,' she added when Gavin accompanied her out to where she had parked her car.

When Kate drove back to Solitaire that afternoon she wondered whether she had not been a little too impulsive in issuing that invitation to Gavin. A vague feeling of uneasiness told her that Rhyno was not going to be pleased, but to the devil with Rhyno, she decided eventually when Solitaire's entrance loomed up ahead of her.

That evening after dinner, while they lingered over coffee at the table, she made her announcement.

'I've invited Gavin to come and have dinner with us on Friday evening,' she said with the light of an anticipated battle flickering in her sapphire blue eyes.

Aunt Edwina opened her mouth to say something, but Rhyno forestalled her with an abrupt, 'You've been seeing him?'

'I met him quite by chance this afternoon while I was out shopping, and he invited me to have tea with him,' she answered truthfully as she withstood Rhyno's narrowed, angry gaze.

'Do you think it's wise?'

'Do you mean inviting Gavin here, or having tea with him in town?' she mocked him, but her mockery was wasted on Rhyno, for his expression remained shuttered.

'Both, I should say.'

Her chin rose defiantly. 'Being married to you, Rhyno, doesn't mean that I have to ignore the existence of my friends.'

'I wouldn't dream of suggesting such a thing,' he replied smoothly, but Kate was instantly aware of that undercurrent of controlled anger in his voice, and she chose to ignore it.

'I'm glad you're taking it that way,' she replied sarcastically, ignoring Aunt Edwina's warning signals.

'I dare say you wouldn't have any objection if I invite Barbara Owen to join us that same evening?'

Kate was momentarily deflated. Of all things she had never expected this, but she recovered her composure swiftly, and said brightly, 'No objection at all.'

'That's settled, then,' he agreed, his expression ominous as he pushed back his chair and got to his feet. 'I'll give her a call and issue the invitation.'

He walked out of the dining hall and closed the door firmly behind him. For a few seconds after his departure there was absolute silence in the room, then Aunt Edwina said reprovingly, 'I hope you realise that what you're doing could only lead to trouble.'

Kate's brows rose a fraction. 'Good heavens, Aunt Edwina, since when is it wrong to invite one's friends over for dinner one evening?'

'Mutual friends, yes,' her aunt agreed anxiously, 'but you know what Gavin has meant to you in the past, and even I know that Barbara Owen was Rhyno's . . .'

'Mistress?' Kate filled in for her aunt when she paused uncomfortably.

Edwina shrank visibly from the word. 'I wouldn't know about that, but I do know that he saw her often.'

'Don't look so worried, Aunt Edwina,' Kate laughed unconcernedly. 'I'm quite convinced we shall spend a highly entertaining evening together.'

Aunt Edwina looked doubtful, and some of her doubt spilled over on to Kate when, later that evening, she lay in bed and wondered just what she had hoped to achieve by inviting Gavin to Solitaire. Surely, as she had said to Rhyno, there was no need for them to ignore the existence of their friends, but why, then, did she have this pinched feeling in her chest at the thought of Barbara Owen coming to Solitaire?

She pondered this question until late that night, but the answer evaded her. She heard Rhyno's footsteps coming down the passage, and moments later there was a strip of light beneath the dressing-room door. She listened to him moving about as she had done almost every night since their marriage, but on this occasion he seemed exceedingly restless for some reason. Long after he had showered she could still hear him moving about, and she found his restlessness infectious. She thought she heard him pause once beside the door, and her heart seemed to leap into her throat, but he resumed his pacing a moment later, and it was some time after midnight before he switched off his light and went to bed.

The silence enveloped Kate, and settled her nerves. She

sighed deeply and rolled over on to her side, hoping to go
to sleep, but her thoughts continued to revolve around
Rhyno and Barbara Owen. Were they lovers, or merely
friends? The latter was highly unlikely, Kate decided at
length. Rhyno's virile masculinity was undeniable, and
Barbara Owen was an extremely attractive woman. Put
two elements like that together, and a platonic relationship wouldn't stand a chance.

The thought of Rhyno making love to Barbara made
Kate squirm inwardly. It had never troubled her before,
but for some unknown reason it troubled her now, and it
was a thought she preferred not to dwell on.

Rhyno would be a masterful lover! The thought came
unbidden into her mind, forcing her to recall the feel of
his hard body against her own, and the bruising intimacy
of his mouth against hers. In his anger his arms had been
like a crushing vice about her, but what, she wondered
crazily, would it feel like to have those strong hands
caressing her instead of dishing out punishment?

She was venturing into dangerous territory, she warned
herself when she felt her pulse quicken. If the mere
thought of Rhyno's caresses could do this to her, then
heaven help her if it ever became reality for some unlikely
reason.

Kate felt nervous and edgy all day Friday, and instead of
looking forward to the evening, she began to dread it. She
dressed with care, convinced that she was going to dislike
Barbara Owen intensely, and determined not to be overshadowed, but instead she found her utterly charming and
pleasant when they met.

Dark-haired and green-eyed, she had a tall, shapely
figure which would make her the envy of most models.
She was sophisticated and beautiful, and Kate concluded
her assessment of this woman by guessing her age some-

where between twenty-five and thirty.

'I can't tell you how thrilled I was to receive Rhyno's invitation,' she told Kate in her warm, honeyed voice soon after her arrival. 'I've heard so much about Solitaire and its superb wines, but I never dreamed I would one day actually have the opportunity of seeing this historic house.'

Gavin, who had never made a secret of the fact that old houses bored him to tears, asked with some surprise, 'Do old, historic houses interest you, Miss Owen?'

'They fascinate me,' Barbara confessed at once. 'They possess a character and nobility one could never find anywhere else.'

'If you're interested then I'm sure my niece would take you on a quick tour of the house before dinner,' Aunt Edwina suggested, and Barbara's eager glance swung in Kate's direction.

'Would you, Kate?'

'I'd be happy to,' Kate replied a little stiffly and, conscious of Rhyno's dark gaze resting on her, she rose to her feet. 'Would you excuse us, please?' she murmured to Gavin.

Kate led the way from the living-room and showed Barbara through the house, explaining the architecture and the layout as they went along. She pointed out where improvements and alterations had been made over the years and, no matter how much she tried, she could not fault the genuine interest Barbara displayed in Solitaire's homestead. Her questions were intelligent and ... *dammit* ... Kate was actually beginning to like her!

'The kitchen was originally situated in this spot, but it was destroyed by fire in 1785, along with the servants' quarters,' Kate explained when they stepped into the open courtyard which led off the existing kitchen, and a little spark of devilment made her add: 'The charred remains of the three Malay servants were supposedly buried under this stone floor, and some people believe they still roam about restlessly at night.'

Barbara shivered visibly. 'Good heavens!'

'Don't allow Kate to frighten you with her ghost stories,' Rhyno's deep voice spoke behind them, and there was a glitter of anger in his eyes when they swung round to face him.

'You were only teasing, were you?' Barbara laughed, seeking confirmation from Kate.

'Yes,' Kate admitted with a reluctant smile. 'The fire was real, also the death of the Malay servants, but they were buried a considerable distance from here.'

'Thank goodness for that!' Barbara exclaimed humorously.

'They're waiting for us to start dinner,' Rhyno announced, linking Barbara's arm through his and adding with unfamiliar concern, 'I hope Kate hasn't impaired your appetite with similar stories as weird as the one I overheard?'

'I made use of one of my father's amusing but untrue anecdotes,' Kate intervened, an unfamiliar ache in her throat as she glanced at the woman walking between Rhyno and herself. 'I'm sorry.'

'Oh, don't apologise, Kate,' Barbara laughed lightly. 'You told it most convincingly, and the amusing part is that I actually believed you.'

Kate's glance met Rhyno's, but unlike Barabara he was not amused by Kate's little prank. He looked, in fact, extremely annoyed, and his oddly protective manner towards Barbara Owen somehow intensified that ache in Kate's throat, forcing her to swallow in an effort to ease it.

'I thought you were never coming back,' Gavin whispered to Kate when she reached his side, but Aunt Edwina rose from her chair before Kate could reply.

'Shall we go through to the dining hall?'

The evening assumed nightmare qualities for Kate. Facing Rhyno across the length of the table, she was conscious of the way he looked at Barbara Owen, and the ease with which they conversed with each other. Why it should have bothered her, she could not imagine, but it triggered off something within her that made her behave towards Gavin in a way which could almost have been termed as flirting.

Rhyno's dark eyes glared at her from time to time across the table, but she merely stared back with a certain insolence before allowing herself to be drawn into a conversation with Gavin once again. Through it all Aunt Edwina remained the perfect hostess, but Kate, who knew her so well, noticed the disapproval in every line of her face, and she knew that the disapproval was directed at herself.

When, at last, they retired to the living-room to finish off the superb dinner with one of Solitaire's best wines, it was Aunt Edwina who explained to Barbara how wine had been made in the early days when she had been a young girl, and she spoke reminiscently of the gaiety of the wine festivals which had been held on Solitaire in her youth. Rhyno later explained the newer, more modern methods, and Kate could not help thinking that they had a totally enthralled audience in Barbara Owen, who apparently could not hear enough of the winemaking activities on the estate.

In need of a dose of fresh air, Kate did not protest when Gavin enticed her out on to the terrace, and it was there that he remarked curiously, 'I didn't know you were on friendly terms with Barbara Owen.'

Kate sighed inwardly. Was there no way of escaping from that woman? she wondered irritably, but her voice was calm and noncommittal when she said: 'I actually met her for the first time this evening.'

'I see,' Gavin muttered, then he drew Kate to his side and asked in a conspiratorial manner, 'Wasn't there something on the go between her and Rhyno before your marriage?'

'I suppose the same thing that was on the go between you and me,' Kate replied with a tight smile.

Gavin drew a little away from her to stare at her in the darkness. 'You believe they were just friends?'

'Oh, come on, Gavin,' she laughed softly and convincingly. 'Is there any reason why I should think differently?'

'No reason at all,' Gavin smiled, turning her to face him, and his appreciative glance travelled over her, taking in her full-skirted dress with the sash around her slim waist, and the smoothness of her bare shoulders in the moonlight. His hands tightened on her arms, and his voice was a little rough as he said: 'You look lovely tonight.'

'Yes, she certainly does,' Rhyno's voice made them jerk apart guiltily, and the next moment Kate found herself trapped against Rhyno's side with his arm heavy and possessive about her waist. 'Marriage suits her, don't you agree with me, Gavin?' he asked in a voice that sounded friendly on the ears, but sent a chill coursing up Kate's spine.

'I agree with you,' Gavin replied smoothly, covering up his embarrassment with admirable swiftness.

There was an awkward little silence while Kate stood stiffly in the circle of Rhyno's arm. She wanted to thrust him from her, but she knew she dared not, then he said in that dangerously convivial tone, 'There's still plenty of wine left inside, if you'd like to fill up your glass.'

'Thank you, I will,' Gavin muttered, and Kate could not help noticing that he looked relieved at being allowed to escape.

The moment they were alone on the terrace Kate said coldly, 'Kindly remove your arm.'

'Certainly,' said Rhyno, but he did not release her entirely. His fingers bit into her wrist, and she was jerked deeper into the shadows where they could not be seen. Before she could open her mouth to utter a protest he had caught hold of her shoulders, jerking her up against him with a force that literally knocked the breath from her body, and she found herself staring up into eyes that were glittering with fury in the moonlight. 'You started this game, Kate,' he warned in a voice that sounded like the low rumble of thunder, 'but play it by the rules, or you might find yourself indulging in a game of a totally different calibre!'

'And what exactly do you mean by that?' she demanded when she managed to get her breath back.

'Work it out for yourself, but just remember one thing . . .' His hands tightened on her shoulders as he paused, then he added savagely, 'I won't be made a fool of.'

Kate stared up at him with an incredulous expression in her wide eyes. 'I believe you're threatening me?'

'You're dead right, I am!'

His thighs were hard against her own, and his hands on her shoulders seemed intent upon crushing the fragile bones beneath the skin, but for one crazy, heart-stopping moment she forgot the pain and longed to feel his lips against her own. She felt his breath on her face, and closed her eyes, but then she was thrust from him with a force that made her utter a startled little cry as she stumbled away from him.

Humiliation stung her cheeks when they returned to the living-room, but she could not help thinking that, if it had been Barbara out there in the moonlight with him, he would not have behaved so harshly, and somehow this irrational thought had the power to hurt her.

Barbara and Gavin left almost simultaneously that evening, and when Kate finally went to bed she decided that the evening had been a failure in every respect. She had prepared herself to dislike Barbara, but instead she had found herself doing exactly the opposite. Barbara Owen was cultured, well versed in most subjects, and she was beautiful, and seeing Rhyno and Barbara together made Kate realise how very much they complemented each other.

That ache was back in her throat, and there was something else, too, which she was forced to admit to herself. *She was jealous!*

'Oh, hell,' she muttered fiercely into the darkness. 'I'm damned if I'll allow myself to fall in love with Rhyno!'

She was fired with determination in this respect, but she had a sinking feeling that her heart might let her down in a moment of desperate need.

CHAPTER SIX

LIFE on Solitaire settled into a rigid pattern which was not exactly dull, but neither was it pleasing. During the week Kate helped where she could with the accounts, or with the despatching of wine in the cellars, and at weekends she usually invited Gavin, Barbara, and Naomi van der Bijl to Solitaire. They would have a *braai*, play tennis, go for long walks, or simply sit around enjoying the fading warmth of the autumn sun. It was one way of continuing her friendship with Gavin, but it was also a way of discovering what Barbara meant to Rhyno.

Barbara had a way of coaxing from Rhyno those rare smiles which transformed his rock-like features in a way that made Kate's heart leap oddly in her breast, and on many occasions she had found herself fighting against an intense longing for something she could not even explain to herself.

She sighed and closed the magazine she had been trying to read. What was the use of pretending to be engrossed when she had not taken in more than a half dozen words?

The rustle of paper made Edwina Duval glance up from her knitting, and the light of the reading lamp accentuated the wrinkles on the once smooth features as she remarked sternly, 'I suppose we're going to have a house full of guests again this weekend.'

'I don't think I'll invite anyone this time,' Kate replied, but what she did not say was that she could no longer bear to watch the easy familiarity between Rhyno and Barbara.

'Thank heaven for that!' Edwina sighed, returning to

her knitting with a less severe expression on her face.

Kate sat for a moment studying the nimble fingers, the slender figure, and the greying hair which had been braided and twisted into a knot in the nape of her aunt's neck. For twenty years this woman had been mother and aunt to her, but for the first time in her life she found herself studying her aunt in a disturbingly different way.

'Why did you never marry and have a family of your own, Aunt Edwina?' she asked suddenly, and Edwina lowered her knitting abruptly to stare at her niece with a puzzled expression in her eyes.

'You've never asked me that before.'

'Perhaps it's because I've selfishly never considered that you were entitled to as much happiness as anyone else. You were always there; the stern mother, and the lovable aunt, and it never crossed my mind that it should be any different.' Kate's glance sharpened. 'Did you forsake your own personal happiness to look after Daddy and myself?'

'No, I didn't,' Edwina shook her head firmly and smiled. 'There was a man once, but in the end he married someone else, and although I've always been perfectly free to marry whom I pleased, no one else has ever appealed to me in that way.' Her grey eyes danced with hidden mirth. 'Does that answer your question?'

'It does,' Kate smiled, feeling extraordinarily relieved for some reason, and, dropping her magazine on to the floor beside her chair, she rose to her feet and hugged her aunt with a warmth and spontaneity stemming from childhood days. There was a lump in her throat, and her eyes filled with unexpected tears as she kissed the cool cheek and whispered 'I think I'll go for a walk.'

It was a dark night, and the chill of winter was in the air as Kate stepped out of the house. She pushed her hands into the pockets of her short leather jacket, and walked on aimlessly until she glimpsed a light in the cellars. What

was Rhyno doing there at this time of night? Curious to
find out, she quickened her pace, and took a short cut
through the shrubs towards the well-trodden path leading
from the house.

She found Rhyno in the underground cellars beside one
of the vats, and there was a glass in his hand which he
held up towards the light. Kate brushed her hair out of
her eyes, and it was what she saw in that glass that shot
her blood-pressure up several degrees.

He turned at the sound of her light footsteps on the
concrete floor, and the familiar smell of fermented grapes
and ageing wine was all around her as she demanded
coldly, 'Since when do we produce a Rosé?'

'As of next year, when it will be bottled and ready for
marketing,' Rhyno replied, sniffing at the blended wine
with infuriating calmness. 'It's time Solitaire added a
Rosé to its list of quality wines.'

'That's your opinion, I suppose.'

'It was originally your father's opinion, but I agreed
with him, and he allowed me to do the blending.'

Kate bristled suddenly with anger. 'Why wasn't I
told?'

'You showed very little interest in the wine cellars
during my first eighteen months here on the estate,'
Rhyno accused harshly. 'Perhaps that's why your father
never told you.'

'*You* could have told me.'

His mouth twisted cynically. 'When, Kate, did you ever
give me the opportunity, or sufficient encouragement, to
tell you anything?'

The truth stung, but she was determined not to show
it. 'I suppose if I hadn't walked in here this evening I
would never have known a thing about what was actually
going on here in the cellars,' she said coldly.

'Stop looking for an argument, Kate, and give me your

honest opinion,' he sighed, almost thrusting the glass into her hand.

'Well, what do you know?' she smiled sarcastically, her fingers tightening about the stem of the glass. 'The *oh-so-clever* Rhyno van der Bijl is actually asking for my lowly opinion!'

'I've never pretended to be anything that I'm not, so cut that out!'

His thundering voice echoed in the rafters, and filled her with shame. Whatever else Rhyno might be, he was not a pretentious man who flaunted his highly specialised qualifications and knowledge of viticulture in front of others, and she lowered her gaze before his as she murmured, 'I'm sorry.'

He brushed aside her apology with an impatient gesture of his hand. 'Taste the wine, and tell me what you think of it.'

Kate obeyed, raising the glass first to her nose to sniff at it. 'It has a delicate bouquet,' she admitted reluctantly, but when she took a small mouthful and swivelled it round her tongue before swallowing, she could not withhold her honest opinion. 'Hm . . . it's clean, well balanced, and with plenty of body, I should say. It tastes promising.'

He removed the glass from her fingers and studied it against the light once more. 'I've entered it in the wine show next month.'

'You're crazy!' she gasped incredulously.

His eyebrows rose a fraction above mocking eyes. 'Because I believe this wine has potential?'

'Because you're wasting your time,' she corrected sharply, and her voice rose faintly in agitation. 'What happens when you take over La Reine? What if you decide to produce your own wines independently, and where does that leave Solitaire when La Reine possesses the essence of this Rosé—or do you intend to market it eventually under your own label?'

'La Reine's wine has been marketed under the Solitaire label for over twenty years, and I see no reason to change that.' He placed the glass on an upturned barrel and thrust his hands into the pockets of his brown, corded pants. 'Unless, of course, you have plans to bar my produce from your cellars once our marriage is over.'

She managed to sustain his bold, challenging gaze, and smiled faintly. 'Don't put ideas into my head.'

'Kate . . .' His hands emerged from his pockets and for one heart-stopping moment she thought he was going to take her in his arms, but he merely gestured vaguely, and asked with a hint of irritation in his deep voice, 'Do you have to have Gavin Page here as often as you do?'

Antagonism emerged from her inexplicable disappointment, and her voice held a hint of sarcasm when she said: 'I've always made a point of also inviting Barbara Owen, or haven't you noticed?'

'I've noticed.' Those glittering hard eyes held hers captive. 'I've also noticed that you've done your best to tie up our weekends these past weeks, as if you're afraid you might have to spend some time alone with me.'

'Don't be silly,' she denied hotly, hoping he would not notice the guilty flush staining her cheeks. 'I enjoy Gavin's company, and I have every reason to believe that you feel the same way about Barbara.'

'I don't deny that I find Barbara's company enjoyable,' he replied without hesitation, sending those now familiar little darts through her. 'She's a sensible, intelligent woman with a warm, passionate nature, and we can have a conversation without her becoming waspish for no reason at all.'

'How nice for you,' Kate remarked acidly. 'You will at least have her passionate warmth to sustain you through the months ahead, and if I'm waspish then you know where to go to have the sting soothed away.'

'Dammit, Kate!' He was beside her in an instant, his hands biting into her shoulders through the leather jacket, and his face was a harsh, impenetrable mask above her. 'You're behaving like a petulant, infuriating child, and the temptation to put you across my knee has never been stronger!'

Her eyes flashed blue fire up at him even though her senses were quiveringly alert to his nearness. 'Do that, Rhyno, and I shall hate you till I draw my last breath,' she hissed through her teeth.

'Will you, Kate?'

There was a dangerous glitter in his eyes, and the roughness of his knitted sweater was beneath her palms as she tried to thrust him from her, but her wrists were seized and her arms were twisted helplessly behind her back. The touch of his hard body against her own set off a vibration within her long before his free hand slipped inside her jacket, and underneath the blouse she had not bothered to tuck into her slacks.

Her breath caught in her throat when that warm, rough hand touched her flesh, and she quivered with a strange mixture of excitement and fear. She found herself gazing hypnotically up into his dark eyes, and saw something there that made her heart beat hard and fast against her ribs.

'Let me go,' she ordered in a voice that should have been cool and unruffled, but instead it sounded shockingly unsteady.

'You ought to be taught a lesson, and I have a feeling that I'm the one to do so,' Rhyno smiled twistedly, his fingers carrying out a series of skilful little caresses along the hollow of her spine that shot tiny fire darts along her veins.

Never before had she found herself in such a dangerous

situation of wanting a man's touch, and knowing that she dared not allow it. Her mind warned against it, but her body responded like a musical instrument in the hands of a master, and an odd weakness invaded her limbs.

'Don't do that!' she begged frantically, struggling in his grasp, but her efforts merely succeeded in making her more aware of thrusting hips and muscled thighs that seemed to be grinding into her mercilessly to induce a melting sensation that intensified the emotions clamouring through her.

'Is it fear that's making your heart beat so fast, or is there some other reason for it?' he asked softly, his eyes on that tell-tale pulse at the base of her throat which was beating so madly, and her face became suffused with angry colour.

'Damn you, Rhyno, let go of me!'

'In a moment,' he promised, his breath fanning her cheek as he lowered his head, 'but not before I've carried out a little experiment.'

She opened her mouth to berate him, and in that moment he captured the full moistness of her lips with his. Rhyno's intimate invasion of her mouth sent a shudder of emotion through her which she would have given anything to suppress, but it was nothing compared to the alien sensations rippling through her when the front catch of her bra snapped beneath his fingers moments before that large hand cupped the smooth swell of her breast. Clinging to her sanity was virtually impossible. She was drugged by his kisses, and his 'tantalising, feather-light caresses made the blood flow through her veins with a fiery sweetness. She was in the grip of an intoxicating madness, like someone who had had too much wine to drink, and when her wrists were no longer imprisoned she raised her hands to his shoulders, her fingers curling into them for support as well as the sheer pleasure of acquainting herself with their muscled hardness beneath the roughness of his sweater.

He caressed her freely now, his lips and hands drawing from her a response which was almost frightening in its intensity. If there was a lesson to be learned in this, then she was learning it with alarming swiftness. Rhyno's lips seemed to devour hers with a heated passion that seared through her like a flame, igniting a fire within her which he fanned with those maddeningly sensual caresses. Her breasts grew taut beneath the skilful manipulation of his fingers, making her desire known to him in no uncertain manner, and for that one brief moment in time she did not care, then sanity returned with a stinging clarity as Barbara Owen's lovely features leapt into her dulled mind, and Kate was instantly filled with a revulsion which was mainly directed at herself, but it was a revulsion tinged with shame.

'For God's sake, Rhyno, stop it!' she cried in a voice that sounded hoarse, and unfamiliar to her own ears as she thrust him from her and, caught offguard, he released her. A strange fire leapt in his eyes, but other than that he gave her the impression that he had remained emotionally untouched, and she hated him with a new intensity at that moment while she stood there fighting to regain the composure she had lost so completely. 'I suggest you save this kind of thing for Barbara. She may appreciate it, but I certainly don't!'

She saw his hands clenching at his sides, and saw the muscles standing out along the side of his jaw as if he were keeping his anger in check. 'You're a little spitfire, Kate, and it's going to take someone far stronger than Gavin to keep you in check.'

'Someone like you, for instance?' she snapped furiously.

'Someone like myself, yes, but I'm not applying for the position, you little shrew.' His dark, narrowed eyes flicked over her with a certain insolence, taking in her flushed cheeks, her quivering lips still swollen from his kisses, and they lingered at the opening of her blouse where a button had come undone to reveal the enchanting cleft between her breasts. The flush on her cheeks deepened, and her hand rose automatically, her fingers fumbling the button into position, but her action merely invited his mockery and contempt. 'You possess none of the qualities I admire in a woman, and I doubt if you ever will.'

Kate felt for a moment as if she were on fire from her head down to her toes, then a terrible coldness shook through her, but it was not the fear of further humiliation that made her turn and flee from the cellars. She had never felt more like giving way to a fit of uncontrollable weeping, and that would have been the final humiliation. Little sobs tore at her throat as she ran back to the house in the darkness, and it was not until she reached the privacy of her room that she gave way entirely to the choking tears.

It was late that night when Rhyno returned to the house, and it was later still when Kate saw the strip of light disappear beneath the dressing-room door. Her tears had long since dried on her cheeks, but her thoughts were in too much of a turmoil to sleep. It was not in her nature to lapse into fits of irrational weeping, but then neither was it in her nature to allow men to touch her the way Rhyno had touched her. She had been kissed before, and she had always prided herself on being in complete command of the situation, but in the cellars that evening Rhyno had taken command, and she had been mentally and physically powerless to resist until that moment when sanity had returned to her, in the form of Barbara Owen.

She did not doubt his low opinion of her, he had made that perfectly clear when he had said: 'You possess none of the qualities I admire in a woman, and I doubt if you ever will.'

Kate turned her face into the pillow to stifle a groan. She not only felt cheap, but she was certain that Rhyno considered her in that light, and it had hurt beyond all imagination to hear him reject her so cruelly. She felt confused and bewildered, her mind turning away from the obvious reason for her misery, but when tiredness finally enveloped her it somehow tore down the barriers she had erected with such specific care, and she found herself facing the unpalatable truth.

She was in love with Rhyno.

She had been attracted to him from the very first moment she had looked into his dark, mocking eyes. She had seen the challenge lurking there, and she had accepted it. She had consciously and subconsciously fought against that fatal attraction; she had resented, despised, and had often ridiculed him, but he had stood firm and unperturbed. Their arguments had always ended in her defeat, and now, where the involvement of her heart was concerned, she had been defeated once again. She loved a man who openly despised her as much as she had always professed to despise him, and she wished, for the first time, that she could stretch this year of marriage into an eternity, but the wheel of time would turn relentlessly, and it was Barbara Owen he would turn to the moment the stipulations in her father's will had been fulfilled.

The Stellenbosch wine show was in progress, and Kate was there with Rhyno on that cold June night in the winery's banquet hall when the results were made known. Solitaire had won seven gold medals and four superior awards, while Rhyno's Rosé had been judged the most promising new blend of the year. It was truly an occasion which called for a celebration, but Kate had never felt less inclined in that direction.

While Rhyno, in particular, was being congratulated, Kate remained silent, almost withdrawn, and it was only when they arrived back at Solitaire that she turned to face him in the living-room, and said without rancour, 'Thank you, Rhyno.'

'Thank you?' he queried with raised eyebrows, handing her a glass of wine before he poured one for himself and sat down in the vacant chair beside the fire.

'For upholding the standard of Solitaire's wines,' she explained, wanting desperately to break through that barrier of cold animosity which had existed between them since that night he had kissed her in the cellars.

'My dear Kate,' Rhyno began with a hint of tolerance in his voice as he brushed a speck of dust from the sleeve of his dark suit, 'most of the credit goes to your father.'

'Most of it, perhaps, but not all of it,' she conceded, lowering her gaze before his, and staring into the crimson liquid in the glass which she clutched between nervous fingers. 'Your Rosé is well on the way to becoming a gold medallist.'

'It's generous of you to say so.'

The derisive mockery in his voice made her glance up at him, and she risked a smile. 'I'm in a generous mood this evening.'

'Are you?'

'Don't look so suspicious,' she laughed softly, taking a sip of her wine to steady her ridiculous nervousness before she added humorously, 'Even a shrew can be generous at times.'

'Are you flirting with me, Kate?' he asked, his eyes intent upon her face while his mouth twisted with mocking derision, and the laughter within her died instantly.

'To flirt with the devil is to court disaster,' she replied stonily, her fingers tightening about the stem of the glass to hide the fact that they were shaking. 'I was trying to be friendly, but I don't suppose you'll believe that.'

The living-room was silent except for the crackling of the log fire, and the ticking of the old-fashioned clock on the mantelshelf. Kate's nerves felt as if they were being stretched to breaking point, then Rhyno asked abruptly, 'Do you associate me with the devil?'

'Sometimes,' she admitted with a sinking feeling in her breast, then she abruptly changed the subject. 'I miss my father this evening. He would have sat here in this chair, and he would have had every right to look proud and satisfied with himself . . . and with you.'

Rhyno's eyes flickered strangely beneath the straight, dark brows. 'Don't exclude yourself, Kate.'

'What you said a few weeks ago was true,' she found herself confessing. 'I did withdraw myself from the activities on the estate after your arrival.'

'That shouldn't stop you from feeling proud and self-satisfied.'

'I haven't, in all honesty, earned the right,' she grimaced.

'You made up for your lapse this season.'

She studied him intently, but his chiselled features gave nothing away, except perhaps for that very slight softening about his harsh mouth which sent a little warmth spiralling through her. 'I believe you're actually trying to comfort me!'

'You find that strange?'

'As strange as you must have found the thought of my wanting to be friendly,' she smiled hesitantly.

'We could never be friends, Kate.'

'No, I suppose not.' Her smile froze on her lips as she dropped into that black pit of despaire and, placing her glass on the table beside her chair, she got to her feet and draped her coat about her shoulders as she walked away from the fire. At the door she turned to glance back at Rhyno where he sat in his chair with his long legs stretched out before him, and in the flickering light of the fire his features assumed an added touch of cruelty. Their eyes met and held for a brief second, then his gaze slid over her, and she quivered almost as if he had caressed her physically. Afraid of being made a fool of, she turned away, and said an abrupt, 'Goodnight.'

She could not sleep that night. She felt like a spring which had been wound up too tight, and she tossed about in bed, her thoughts leaping wildly from one subject to the other. Rhyno had considered her manner flirtatious. Had she perhaps been flirting with him subconsciously? No, never! If only her father were here, then none of this would have been necessary. Oh, *damn*! If only she could go to sleep!

The moonlight filtered through the trees outside her window, and the shadows danced against the wall like grotesque little men, darting, leaping in tune to the sighing wind. Kate observed this display intently, trying to make her mind a blank in order to induce sleep, but she failed, and finally got up to put on her dressing-gown. She walked through the darkened house towards the kitchen, the soft mules on her feet barely making a sound, and when she snapped on the kitchen light she stood blinking for a moment until her eyes became accustomed to the sudden brightness. He gaze shifted towards the electric clock against the wall. Twelve-thirty! She grimaced and, taking out a saucepan, poured milk into it and placed it on the stove.

'Can't you sleep?'

She swung round, her eyes wide and dark in her pale face. Rhyno stood leaning against the door jamb, his hands thrust into the pockets of his black towelling robe, and his dark hair falling untidily across his broad forehead.

'No, I—I guess the excitement was too much,' she managed unsteadily, grasping at the first excuse that entered her head, and turned away from that fatal magnetism which seemed to reach out and enfold her. 'Would you like a mug of cocoa?'

'If it's not too much trouble.'

Ultra-sensitive for some inexplicable reason, she thought she detected sarcasm in his voice, and her temper flared. 'I wouldn't have asked if I'd——' She paused abruptly, bit her lip, and sighed. 'Why are we always snapping at each other?'

'You started.'

'Only because you were sarcastic,' she defended herself.

His eyebrows rose in sardonic amusement. 'Sarcastic? Me?'

'You know you were, and don't deny it,' she accused, her anger rising again as swiftly as it had subsided.

'My dear Kate——'

'And don't speak to me in that lordly tone!' she interrupted sharply.

They glared at each other in silence for interminable seconds, then Rhyno pushed himself away from the door and walked towards her with a look on his face which she could not quite define.

'Perhaps you would prefer it if I didn't speak at all,' he said, pausing directly in front of her and making her intensely aware of the unmistakable virility encased in the height and breadth of him. 'Perhaps there's a more satisfactory way we could communicate.'

'What do you mean?' she asked, her heart hammering hard against her ribs.

'Do you need to be told?' he smiled down at her cynically, and too late she saw the danger lurking in his eyes.

'No, Rhyno!' she gasped protestingly, but one arm had

already slipped about her waist to clamp her hard against him, and a hand was in her long silky hair, bunching into a fist at the nape of her neck and preventing her from evading those descending lips.

She steeled herself to endure his brutality, but the sensual pressure of his mouth against hers tore down the barriers of her resistance, and her lips parted in response beneath his before she could stop herself. Her hands clung to his shoulders, aware of the rippling muscles beneath the towelling material, and even as her mind warned her to take care, her body responded to that hand moving in a slow caress down her back. Rhyno moulded her to him effortlessly, his lips straying to her small ear, her pulsating throat, and lower still to the opening of her dressing-gown. His mouth was warm, as warm as his hands, which seemed to be burning her through the silky material, and every nerve and pulse in her body was beginning to throb with a wildness that inflamed her with the most exquisite sensations.

She was released abruptly, and she stared up at Rhyno a little dazedly to see him tilting his head at a listening angle. It was only then that she heard the footsteps approaching the kitchen and, aware that she not only felt but looked emotionally disturbed, she turned towards the stove and made a pretence of concentrating on the saucepan of milk.

'What's going on in this house?' Aunt Edwina demanded sharply. 'At one o'clock in the morning you should both be asleep, but instead you're walking up and down, opening and closing doors, and now I find you in the kitchen!' She paused effectively, but when neither of them responded, she added in a grumbling voice, 'How am I supposed to get a few hours of rest with all this activity going on in the house?'

'We apologise, Aunt Edwina, but it's the excitement,'

Rhyno replied, explaining briefly what had occurred at the wine show.

'This calls for a celebration, it seems,' Aunt Edwina announced, seating herself at the table. 'If you're making cocoa, Kate, then I'll have some as well.'

Kate sighed inwardly. 'Yes, Aunt Edwina.'

'Tell me everything, Rhyno,' Edwina insisted, gesturing him into a chair close to her while Kate poured an extra amount of milk into the saucepan.

While Rhyno and Aunt Edwina discussed the show, Kate made the cocoa and tried desperately not to reveal how shaken she was by what had occurred between Rhyno and herself mere seconds before Aunt Edwina had entered the kitchen. Each time he kissed her was a revelation in itself, and it left her with her emotions as scattered as the leaves beneath the trees when the wind had whirled through it. Rhyno, it seemed, had remained unmoved, and Kate finally observed him over the rim of her mug while he talked to her aunt. His chiselled features revealed no flaw, and no weakness one could pinpoint. His jaw was square, and set permanently with an inner determination which she had become aware of from their very first meeting. The mouth was stern, despite the hint of sensuality in the lower lip, and her own lips tingled at the memory of that warm mouth against her own.

Almost as if he had been aware of her observation, Rhyno turned his head and their glances collided. Kate's cheeks went pink, and she looked away hastily, cursing herself for being caught staring, but Rhyno continued speaking as if nothing had happened.

'Jacques would have been so proud,' Edwina announced when Rhyno fell silent, then she glanced at him anxiously. 'By the way, Rhyno, there was a call from Barbara this evening, and she asked if you would give her a ring first thing in the morning.'

'Thank you, I'll do that.'

Just like that, Kate thought, not quite sure whether it was anger or jealousy flaring so hotly in her veins. Barbara raised her little finger, and Rhyno came running. It was disgusting, it was degrading, and . . . oh, how Kate wished he would look at her just once as if he liked her!

'Well, I'm off to bed,' said Aunt Edwina, getting to her feet and pushing her chair under the table. 'I need my sleep even if you two don't.'

Kate collected the mugs in silence after Aunt Edwina had left. She rinsed them out and poured water into the saucepan. She felt nervous and edgy with Rhyno watching every move she made, and her heart almost stopped beating when she turned eventually and found his large frame blocking her path towards the door. He had a look in his eyes that told her he had intentions of taking up where they had left off at Aunt Edwina's entrance, but she was not going to fall into that trap again; not while he was still at Barbara Owen's beck and call.

'Don't touch me!' she snapped, stepping beyond the reach of his hands. 'Whatever else you may think of me, I refuse to be your plaything!'

'What's got into you now?' he growled, thrusting his hands into the pockets of his robe and glowering at her from beneath his dark brows.

'Simply this,' she stated coldly. 'I don't wish to be mauled by you again.'

She did not wait to witness the result of her statement and, darting round the opposite side of the table, marched out of the kitchen and left him standing there, but she felt the burning fury of his eyes on her back moments before she slipped out of the door.

CHAPTER SEVEN

KATE was seated behind her father's old desk in the study, sorting through a pile of papers the following morning, when Rhyno opened the door and walked in.

'I have to go away for a few days,' he announced without preamble. 'Do you think you'll manage on your own?'

Kate's cool gaze took in his lean length in the dark grey suit. 'I'm not a helpless, incompetent fool, you know.'

'For heaven's sake, Kate!' he snapped harshly, his eyes darkening with anger. 'I never suggested that you were a helpless, incompetent fool. I merely asked if you thought you could cope.'

'I'll manage perfectly, thank you,' she replied coldly. 'How long will you be away?'

'I'm not sure.' His expression became shuttered. 'Two, maybe three days.'

'I presume it has something to do with Barbara,' she remarked with a casualness that belied the pain she felt as she drove the sword into her own heart.

'That's right.' His eyes burned down into hers, and the next moment he slammed the proverbial door in her face. 'It's a personal matter that doesn't concern you.'

'I don't think you need to enlighten me into the nature of your affair,' she hit back, careless of her choice of words.

There was a brief, ominous silence, then he said mockingly, 'It's good of you to take it so sensibly.'

'Rhyno,' she stopped him on his way to the door, 'I

hope I can rely on you to be discreet?'

Their glances clashed, but Kate did not look away as he approached the desk and placed his hands flat on the surface. 'One day, Kate,' he growled, leaning towards her with a menacing look on his face, 'one day you'll go too far.'

'Are you threatening me again?' she asked, her voice heavy with sarcasm.

'Not threatening,' he contradicted harshly. 'Merely warning you that I'm running low on tolerance.'

'Let's hope that your sojourn with Barbara puts you in a better frame of mind, then.'

'I've no doubt it will,' his voice grated along her raw, quivering nerves. 'I've never known a more soothing person to be with.'

Kate flinched visibly when he slammed the door behind him moments later, and she stared at it miserably for several seconds before she made an attempt to concentrate on her work. Fifteen minutes later she heard Rhyno drive away in his Citroën, and after that she found it impossible to make any sense out of the papers before her. All she could think of was the fact that Rhyno was going off somewhere with Barbara for a few days, and the thought of it drove her slightly mad.

When Aunt Edwina mentioned at the lunch table that she needed a few things in town, Kate was almost relieved at the thought of having something to do and, armed with the list of requirements her aunt had given her, she drove in to Stellenbosch that afternoon. Perhaps there would be time, as well, for that promised visit to Rhyno's mother, she thought. Naomi van der Bijl had that wonderful ability to boost one's morale when it was at its lowest, and that was exactly what Kate needed on that cold, wintry afternoon.

Meeting Gavin in town was a pleasant surprise, and

she did not object when he offered to carry her parcels back to her car for her.

'I saw you only briefly last night at the wine show, Kate,' he said as he closed the boot. 'Are you free to have tea with me this afternoon?'

'I was on my way to Rhyno's mother,' she explained.

'Is she expecting you?' he asked, and when she shook her head he drew her arm through his and said: 'In that case forget about her, and have tea with me instead.'

Gavin was nothing if not persuasive and, quite frankly, she felt in need of his company that afternoon. He ordered tea and scones, and when it arrived Kate poured.

'I've been wanting to have a private chat to you for quite some time,' he said at length when he had devoured the last of the scones. 'Would you give me a straight answer to a few straight questions?'

Kate smiled at him over the rim of her cup. 'This sounds serious.'

'It is, believe me.' He did not return her smile, but merely watched her grimly from across the small table. 'Will you do as I ask?'

'I'll try,' she agreed unsuspectingly.

'Was there something in your father's will that forced you to marry Rhyno?' His glance registered Kate's startled expression, and when she hesitated he added persuasively, 'We're friends, Kate. Surely you can confide in me?'

Torn with indecision, she stared back at him, then she thought, 'Why shouldn't I tell him? He's my friend, as he said, and what, after all, are friends for if not to confide in?'

'My father's will did have something to do with it,' she confessed eventually, wondering vaguely where he had received his information.

'Was that the only way you could get your inheritance?'

'Yes,' she sighed. 'I have to stay married to him for a year before I can claim Solitaire as my own.'

She smothered her feeling of guilt and told herself that it was a relief to be talking to Gavin like this. She had thought once that she might marry him, but now, of course, it was quite out of the question.

Almost as if he had tuned in to her thoughts, Gavin said: 'Will you marry me, Kate? When this year is up, I mean?'

'I can't answer that at the moment, Gavin,' she evaded his question.

'Just tell me you'll consider it when the time comes.'

'Tell him,' a little voice at the back of Kate's mind prompted. 'Tell him not to waste his time hoping.' Kate looked into those serious blue eyes, and somehow she didn't have the heart to disillusion him. 'I'll consider it,' she heard herself say, and she did not draw her hand away when his fingers clasped hers tightly across the table.

'I love you, Kate.'

'Please, Gavin ... don't,' she begged, shrinking from him inwardly. 'I have enough problems at the moment without you making it worse.'

'I'm sorry,' he smiled faintly and released her hand. 'There's just one more question I must ask. Is your marriage to Rhyno ... well, you know what I mean?'

Kate hesitated, aware of Gavin's discomfort, and aware too of the danger in saying too much. She had given Rhyno her word that no one would know the truth about their marriage, but Gavin knew so much already that she decided it would do no harm for him to know it all. She could trust him, she was certain of that, and with this thought in mind, she said: 'Our marriage is no more than a business arrangement.'

'I see.'

A peculiar expression flitted across Gavin's face and, filled with sudden anxiety, she said: 'You will keep it to yourself, won't you?'

'Of course,' he smiled broadly. 'You know you can trust me.'

Kate sighed inwardly with relief, but when she drove herself back to Solitaire some time later she found herself grappling with a feeling of guilt which she could not shake off. Gavin would keep it to himself, of course he would, she told herself. But if Rhyno should ever find out . . .! She shivered at the thought.

That evening, when she sat in front of the living-room fire with Aunt Edwina, she thought about it again, and she wondered suddenly whether it had been a wise thing to confide in Gavin. He would not do anything to hurt her, but . . . could she really trust him? And Rhyno? What would he do if he should find out that she had told Gavin everything?

'When do you expect Rhyno back?' her aunt interrupted her thoughts, and Kate glanced up sharply at the mention of Rhyno's name.

'I don't really know when to expect him,' she replied cautiously. 'Why do you ask?'

'I'd like to spend a few weeks with friends of mine in Cape Town.' Edwina lowered her knitting and smiled at her niece. 'It's warmer there this time of the year, and I think I need a change of scenery.'

'You could go any time you want, Aunt Edwina,' Kate assured her. 'You know I'll be perfectly safe here on my own.'

Edwina shrank visibly from the idea. 'I couldn't do that.'

'Don't be silly, of course you could,' Kate insisted. 'I'll ring the station first thing in the morning and make a booking for you.'

'But, Kate——'

'Don't argue, Aunt Edwina,' Kate interrupted firmly. 'I shouldn't be surprised if Rhyno arrived home some time tomorrow, or the day after anyway.'

Edwina was not at all convinced that leaving Kate alone on Solitaire was the right thing to do, even if it was only for one night, but Kate finally persuaded her to the contrary, and the following morning, after a restless night wondering about Rhyno and Barbara, Kate telephoned the station and managed to get a booking for Aunt Edwina on the train leaving for Cape Town that same afternoon.

Edwina was still protesting when Kate saw her off at the station shortly after lunch that day, but Kate pretended not to hear. Her aunt went off to Cape Town every year for a few weeks during the winter months, and Kate saw no reason why she should delay her departure because of Rhyno's absence from the estate.

Kate was home barely a half hour when the telephone rang and, thinking it might be Rhyno, she almost ran to answer it, but instead she heard Gavin's voice asking, 'Did I see you coming from the direction of the station early this afternoon?'

'Yes, you did,' Kate replied, swallowing down her disappointment, and then, to her dismay, she heard herself explaining that she would be alone on Solitaire until Rhyno returned. She could have kicked herself afterwards, but it was too late, and Gavin was quick to make use of the situation.

'If you're on your own, then perhaps you would consider having dinner with me this evening.'

'I . . . don't know, I——'

'Come on, Kate,' Gavin persisted eagerly. 'It would be preferable to sitting down to a solo meal this evening, surely.'

'I admit that, but——'

'Are you expecting Rhyno to return this evening?'

'I have no idea when to expect him,' she confessed warily.

'Well then?' There was a brief silence, then Gavin added persuasively, 'Shall I call for you at seven?'

Kate hesitated, her subconscious warning against accepting Gavin's invitation, but then she thought, 'Why not?' If Rhyno could be having the time of his life somewhere with Barbara, then why shouldn't she dine out with Gavin?

'Very well,' she said at length. 'I'll be ready at seven.'

The evening out with Gavin was not a success. It was, in fact, a mistake she was to regret before the night was over. Gavin talked at length about leaving the winery and launching himself into his computer business, but Kate barely listened. She felt uneasy and restless, and not at all as relaxed as she had always been in his company.

'I have a funny feeling that you're not with me,' Gavin grinned at her when they had reached the coffee stage, and she looked up at him guiltily.

'I'm sorry, Gavin, but——'.

'You're not worried about something, are you?' he interrupted, his expression sobering.

'No, of course not,' she lied hastily. 'But I think I'd like you to take me home now, if you don't mind.'

'But it's barely ten o'clock,' Gavin exclaimed in astonishment as he glanced at his wrist watch. 'Darling, you can't be serious!'

She wished he wouldn't call her 'darling', but aloud she said: 'Please, Gavin, take me home.'

'If you insist,' he sighed, grimacing as he got to his feet and placed her wrap about her shoulders.

'Don't be angry, Gavin,' she begged finally when they had driven some distance in silence.

'I'm not angry, sweetheart,' he laughed easily. 'Your wish is always my command.'

There was something about his attitude that puzzled her suddenly, but she could not quite decide what it was, and the endearments flowing so easily from his lips were beginning to irritate her intensely.

'Everything still looks the same as when we left,' Gavin remarked when at last he parked his car in front of the house.

'Yes,' Kate agreed with him abruptly.

'Shall I come in just to make sure that everything is all right?'

The note of concern in his voice made her feel guilty and, against her better judgment, she said: 'You could come in and have a quick cup of coffee if you like.'

'I was hoping you'd ask,' Gavin laughed, and linked his arm through hers when they climbed the steps up to the heavy oak door.

The house looked quiet and empty. The lights she had left on earlier that evening were the only lights on at that moment, and it was with a measure of relief that she unlocked the front door and led the way into the living-room.

'Kate . . .' Gavin caught her wrist as she passed him on her way to the kitchen. 'Don't go just yet.'

She glanced up at him in wary silence, not quite liking the look in his eyes, and not quite sure how to handle the situation. He knew too much for her own comfort, and she knew with sudden clarity that it had been a mistake confiding in him, but it was too late now for regrets.

'I haven't really had the opportunity to tell you how lovely you look this evening, and how much I love you,' he continued, and she disliked that hint of insolence in his eyes as they travelled over her.

'Gavin, I don't——'

Her protest was cut short when he pulled her into his arms and silenced her lips with his own. Kate was too stunned at first to react, but when her mind finally grasped the situation she decided it could be dangerous at this point to antagonise Gavin. She had unintentionally placed a weapon in his hands by confessing the truth about her marriage to Rhyno, and the only way to deal with the situation at that precise moment was to remain passive in his arms in the hope that he would soon realise that she was not responding to his passionate embrace.

Something, a sound perhaps, made her struggle against the pressure of Gavin's lips and arms, and when she finally managed to free herself she was horrified at the sight of the man standing framed in the living-room door.

'*Rhyno!*' his name burst from her lips, and the look on his face was enough to make her wish that the floor would cave in beneath her.

'I hate to interrupt this tender scene,' Rhyno smiled twistedly, his eyes on Gavin who stood facing him with a mixture of insolence and bravado on his face. 'Someone ought to remind you, Gavin, that you're poaching on my property.'

'Your property!' Gavin laughed sneeringly, and Kate's eyes widened in absolute terror when he added: 'Kate is no more your property than she is mine!'

'Shut up, Gavin!' she hissed urgently.

'No, Kate,' Rhyno smiled at her coldly, his manner stern and authoritative despite the fact that he was dressed only in his black towelling robe. 'Please let him explain his interesting statement,' he added, turning back to Gavin.

'No explanation is necessary,' Gavin replied, glancing swiftly at Kate when he realised his error.

'If you refuse to give me an explanation, then you must at least clarify your statement,' Rhyno persisted with an ominous look on his hard features.

'This is ridiculous!' Kate intervened nervously.

'Not as ridiculous as you may think, Kate,' Rhyno stated harshly without taking his eyes off Gavin. 'I'm waiting to hear what you have to say, Gavin.'

Gavin went red in the face, then he blurted out angrily, 'Who the hell do you think you are, talking to me like this?'

'I'm Kate's husband,' Rhyno reminded him with a terrifying calmness in his deep voice.

'In name only, yes, and unless you alter your attitude towards me I shall see to it that everyone finds out about it,' Gavin informed him sneeringly, totally oblivious of what he was doing to Kate. 'You don't frighten me, Rhyno van der Bijl. I admit that I don't know all the details, but I'm willing to bet that you're not going to come out of this so-called marriage of yours empty-handed!'

White-faced and wishing at that moment that she could shrivel up and die, Kate saw Rhyno's large fist smack into Gavin's jaw, and the blow sent Gavin sprawling on the carpet with blood oozing from the corner of his mouth.

Kate's own fears were momentarily shelved as she exclaimed in horror, 'Rhyno! For heaven's sake, you've killed him!'

'Get up, Page!' Rhyno thundered, ignoring Kate.

'You'll pay for this, I swear,' Gavin muttered thickly, struggling to his feet, and dabbing lightly at his mouth with his handkerchief which was becoming soaked with his blood.

'I don't somehow think so,' Rhyno contradicted icily, towering head and shoulders above a rather pathetic-looking Gavin. 'Does the name Geoffrey Princeton ring a bell?'

Gavin's colour came and went, but he scowled at Rhyno and snapped, 'I don't know anyone by that name.'

'Don't you?' Rhyno's lips twisted into a savage smile. 'What about the name Gary Parkes?'

'Never heard of him.'

'That's strange,' Rhyno remarked smoothly, taking his pipe out of the pocket of his robe and lighting it with unusual care. 'I happened to be in the office of a friend of mine yesterday. He's in the Cape Town fraud and robbery squad, and it just so happened that he had a very interesting file on his desk.'

The atmosphere was tense in the living-room, and as Kate glanced frowningly from Gavin's white face to Rhyno's large, threatening frame, she felt she would scream if someone did not explain to her what was going on.

'For pity's sake, Rhyno,' she cried in a choked voice, 'what are you talking about?'

Rhyno glanced at her briefly, but it was a look that made her shrink inside with something more than ordinary fear.

'You know, don't you, Page?' Rhyno persisted in that dangerously smooth voice.

'I don't know what you're trying to pin on me,' Gavin spluttered, 'but I tell you it won't work.'

'I don't have to pin anything on you, your file at police headquarters is quite thick enough.'

'Police headquarters?' Kate exclaimed in faintly hysterical confusion. 'Are you mad, Rhyno?'

'Stay out of this, Kate!' Rhyno lashed her savagely, thrusting his pipe into his pocket, and returning his attention to the man before him. 'Geoffrey Princeton, Gary

Parkes, or Gavin Page—I still don't know which one is your real name, but you've made quite a packet over the years by leading wealthy young women up the garden path, wheedling money out of them with talk of starting your own business in which they would become shareholders, and then dropping them flat once they'd given you all they had to give.' Rhyno's large hands shot out and, grasping Gavin by the lapels of his jacket, he lifted him almost off his feet as he demanded fiercely, 'How much did you get out of Kate?'

'Nothing—nothing, I swear,' Gavin stammered hastily, confessing his guilt in no uncertain terms, and his features whitened at the savagery locked up in Rhyno's expression.

'Then it's true?' Kate whispered in disbelief as the truth began to penetrate her numbed brain. 'Gavin, is it true?'

'Answer her, dammit!' Rhyno roared, shaking Gavin like a dog would shake a cat when it seemed that Gavin was not going to reply.

'Yes—yes, it's true,' Gavin admitted thickly, blood dripping from his chin on to his white shirt front.

'Were you going to do the same to me?' Kate questioned, unable to grasp the fact that someone she had liked and trusted could have contemplated anything so vile. 'Is that why you talked so often of your plans to start a computer business?'

'You don't need to doubt that he was planning to deplete your bank balance one way or another, but your marriage to me delayed his plans somewhat,' Rhyno answered for Gavin. 'Isn't that so, Page?'

'Yes,' Gavin admitted dully, then Rhyno thrust him aside.

'Get out of here, Page, and if I were you I'd get right out of this district before that friend of mine in the police department becomes suspicious of my interest in one of his files,' Rhyno warned harshly.

Straightening his jacket, Gavin turned to leave, but at the door he hesitated, and turned. 'Kate, I——'

'Get out before I throw you out!' Rhyno thundered, and Gavin obeyed, almost running from the house to where he had parked his car.

Kate felt her insides lurch sickeningly when she heard his car drive away and, dashing past Rhyno, she almost ran to her room. She felt nauseated at the thought that she could have been so gullible, and all she wanted was to be left alone, but Rhyno entered her room moments later and, venting her anger and disappointment on him, she snapped, 'What do you want? Can't you leave me alone?'

'I haven't finished with you yet, Kate,' he told her in that quite voice that sent shivers of apprehension racing up and down her spine. 'I've taken more from you than I've taken from anyone else in my life, but you've made your final mistake where I'm concerned.'

This is it, Kate thought, pulling herself together from the shock of discovering the truth about Gavin. This was her moment of retribution for breaking her word and confiding in someone she had considered a friend, but she was determined not to let Rhyno guess that she was shaking inwardly with nervousness and fear.

'What are you talking about?' she demanded with a deceptive calmness, meeting the full force of his blazing eyes.

'We made a pact that no one, other than my mother, your aunt, and Hubert Walton would know the true circumstances of our marriage. You broke that pact when you told Gavin Page the truth, and that gives me a free hand to deal with the situation as I see fit.'

'What do you intend to do, Rhyno?' she questioned in an attempt at defiance. 'Thrash me?'

'Nothing as simple as that.' His eyes raked her from

head to foot, and left her feeling oddly naked. 'After tonight, Kate, you'll be lying through your teeth if you tell anyone that our marriage isn't real.'

Kate stared at him with something akin to horror in her eyes. She must have misunderstood him, she told herself, but fear snaked through her, leaving her whiter than before, and shaking. 'You—you can't mean——'

'Yes, I do,' he confirmed, his harsh voice grating along her sensitive nerves. 'When the time comes to end our marriage we shall be filing for a divorce, and not merely seeking an annulment, because we will have been well and truly married.'

'You're mad!' she cried, raising a trembling hand to her throat to ease the tightness.

'Yes, Kate,' he acknowledged sharply, his hands clenched at his sides as he lessened the distance between them. 'I was mad to have thought you would honour our agreement.'

Kate could not believe that he would carry out his threat, but she was taking no chances as she backed away from him. 'Stay away from me, or I'll scream!'

'Scream as much as you wish,' he laughed harshly. 'There's no one here to hear you.'

The crimson curtains were behind her and, white and trembling, she searched frantically for some sign that he was merely trying to frighten her, but his features could very easily have been chiselled out of granite at that moment. She had never seen him look so menacing before, nor so vitally masculine, and her temples were beginning to pound with terror, and something more. She knew herself too well. She would have no defence against an onslaught of this nature, and heaven only knew what he might discover once her treacherous emotions began to dictate her actions.

'If you touch me, Rhyno,' she warned unsteadily,

shrinking inwardly from the blazing fury of his glance, 'if you touch me I shall hate you for as long as I live!'

'Then now's the time to start hating me,' he muttered through his teeth, and his hands, like steel traps, snapped about her arms and jerked her up against him.

'Let me go!' she cried, beating her fists against his chest, but he seemed not to notice, and merely laughed satanically at her efforts to avoid his descending lips. He grasped a fistful of hair at the back of her head, forcing her face out into the open, and her cry of agony was smothered beneath the crushing force of his mouth.

She felt dizzy, her senses swimming, and when that muscled body moved against hers she felt a terrifying weakness invade her limbs. She fought against it mentally and physically, but the zip of her dress gave way beneath the expertise of his hands, and it slid to the floor to lie in a silken heap at her feet.

'For God's sake, Rhyno, don't do this!' she begged at length when he freed her lips to plunder the satiny warmth of her bare shoulder where he had eased off the flimsy straps of her slip and bra. Her fingers bit into his shoulders through the towelling robe in an effort to push him away, but her efforts to escape made her more aware of hard muscles grinding into her slowly yielding flesh.

'Fight all you want, you little wildcat,' he warned throatily close to her ear, 'but tonight you're going to be tamed.'

'You can't do this to me!' she cried almost tearfully as he lifted her effortlessly out of her shoes and urged her towards the bed.

'I can do whatever I please,' he told her savagely, stripping her writhing body down to her skin. 'You're my wife and, God help me, tonight you're going to pay for all the insults I've had to endure!'

'Rhyno . . . don't . . . I beg of you,' she pleaded

hoarsely, her colour coming and going as she gave way at last to her fears.

She tried to cover her nakedness with her hands, but Rhyno was merciless, and spared her nothing as he thrust her backwards on to the bed. He followed her down before she could escape him by rolling off the other side and, pinned down beneath that hard, muscled body, she begged, pleaded, and wept, but he was blind and deaf to everything except the desire for revenge. His mouth finally silenced hers, and forced her into submission.

Kate had never before felt so agonisingly helpless in all her life. His hands were hard on her body, invading her with an intimacy which was devoid of any sign of tenderness, and even though she found herself responding to his ruthless passion, she fought him determinedly to the bitter end. Her nails raked his flesh when she felt him remove his robe, but her breath locked in her throat when she found herself moulded to that lean, hard body. She was, eventually, aware of nothing else except the clean, tantalising scent of his body, the frightening width of his gleaming shoulders above her, and the naked desire in his dark eyes. She prayed that he would put out the light to spare her the final humiliation of having him observe her reactions, but Rhyno was determined to make her pay the supreme penalty, and he devoured her with his eyes and his body, not sparing her until a cry of mingled pain and pleasure burst from her parted, swollen lips.

Afterwards, lying dry-eyed in the darkness while Rhyno slept beside her, Kate felt peculiarly empty. She hated him in a way she had never thought possible for shattering her somewhat childish illusions, and that left her with only an aching dissatisfaction tearing away at her insides. What had occurred between them could not be termed as an act of making love. Love had not been involved at all—only a desire born of vengeance. Making love was surely a blending of mind, body and soul, but while her mind might have been conquered and her body ravaged, her soul had remained untouched. Rhyno had intended to punish her, and he had succeeded in the most diabolical way.

Humiliated and mentally beaten, she finally went to sleep, but it was an uneasy sleep from which she awoke in the night to find herself being caressed with a slow, tantalising intimacy that made her blush in the darkness. She remained perfectly still, too afraid to move or give any indication that she was aware of what was happening, but a soft moan of pleasure escaped her when Rhyno's mouth found the sensitive peak of her breast, and her fingers somehow became locked behind his head in the thick, crispness of his hair.

This time it was breathtakingly different. His love-making raised her out of herself into a realm where nothing existed beyond the waves of sensual pleasure buffeting her exquisitely, raising her higher and higher towards that unknown goal. She could swear eventually that she heard the music of the spheres as those sensations intensified, then she was thrust like helpless flotsam into that unfamiliar world where wave after wave of ecstatic pleasure washed over her until she knew the true meaning of fulfilment.

She emerged slowly from this alien world she had been plunged into, and as their bodies still clung in the aftermath of shared enjoyment, she knew, at last, that she was a woman in the fullest sense. In the silent darkness Rhyno's lips sought hers, and with her arms locked unashamedly about his neck, she returned his kisses with an eagerness she could not hide.

CHAPTER EIGHT

RHYNO was not in the room when Kate woke up the following morning, and she assumed that he had gone out into the vineyards. She did not want to think of what had happened between them, the mere thought of it made her go hot with humiliation and shame, and she dreaded having to face Rhyno in the cold light of day knowing that there was not a part of her body he had not acquainted himself with during the night.

She felt herself blush from the roots of her hair down to her toes and, groaning inwardly, she stepped into the shower, deliberately opening the cold water tap so that the icy spray could cool her heated body. There were bruises on her arms and legs which she had acquired in her efforts to fight him off, but it was nothing compared to the mental bruises which made her wince inwardly.

After a quick breakfast she locked herself up in the study, and kept herself reasonably busy with the large amount of paperwork involved in the management of a wine estate. She desperately needed those few hours to prepare herself mentally for having to face Rhyno again, and when she finally joined him for lunch in the small dining-room which they had begun to use more frequently since her father's death, she complimented herself silently on managing to look outwardly cool and composed.

In khaki pants and thick brown sweater, his shoulders somehow looked broader, and his hips leaner. Despite her efforts, the memory of that hard, muscular body against her own leapt to the surface of her mind, and her heartbeats quickened, sending the flow of blood more rapidly through her veins. 'Damn him!' she thought furiously. He had made her aware of herself as a woman, and of desires she had never known existed. She did not know whether to thank him or to hate him for it, but at the moment she was more inclined to do the latter.

She felt his eyes on her while she toyed with her food, and a mouthful of salad went down like a boulder. At that moment she envied him his ability to behave as though nothing had happened between them and, furious with herself for not being able to do the same, she pushed aside her plate and helped herself to a cup of coffee.

'Are you never going to look at me or speak to me again?' Rhyno's mocking voice quivered along her nerve ends, and the eyes she finally raised to his were twin sapphires of heated fury.

'I wish I didn't have to see you or speak to you again for the rest of my life!'

'It wasn't that bad the second time, was it?'

His reference to the intimacy they had shared made her colour rise sharply, and she lowered her gaze. 'I don't want to talk about it.'

'You enjoyed it as much as I did,' he taunted her.

'Shut up!'

'Do you deny it?'

'No, I don't,' she snapped after a momentary pause, her face rigid with anger and despair. 'But then you're an expert at that sort of thing, and you had had recent practice as well!'

Her arrow hit its mark, and his face darkened ominously. 'Leave Barbara out of this.'

'No, I will not!' she persisted with angry cynicism. 'What will she think when she discovers that you don't only go to bed with her, but with me as well?'

'Unlike you, Kate, I never told Barbara the truth about our marriage.'

'You mean she doesn't object to being your mistress?' she questioned, ignoring his stab. 'Even though you're married and sleeping with your wife?'

The only reply she received was a faint smile, and his apparent calmness simply infuriated her more.

'I knew there had to be a flaw somewhere,' she said icily. 'She was too good to be true.'

'I told you to leave Barbara out of this,' he said with a quiet savagery she could not ignore. 'My relationship with her is something your twisted little mind would never understand.'

That stung, and she winced inwardly. 'The only one around here with a twisted mind is you, Rhyno. And while we're on the subject of twisted minds, how did you find out about Gavin?'

His expression hardened considerably. 'Barbara thought she recognised him as the chap who'd once taken advantage of an old acquaintance of hers, and I took the investigation a little further.'

'Was that why you went to Cape Town?'

'It was one of the reasons,' he replied noncommittally, and hurt and anger seemed to combine inside Kate.

'The other reasons concern only Barbara and yourself, I take it?'

'That's right.'

Being excluded was one thing, but the feeling of having a door slammed in your face was another, and Kate rose from the table abruptly. 'If you'll excuse me, I have work to do.'

Rhyno pushed back his chair and got to his feet. 'I'll give you a lift down to the cellars.'

'I'll walk, thank you,' Kate declined coldly, turning on her heel and marching out of the room.

It was good to feel the breeze in her hair, and the sun on her face, she decided as she stepped out of the house, and she needed to walk off that gnawing ache in her heart.

The vineyards looked sad in winter. Nature had stripped the vines naked of their foliage, but expert, caring hands had pruned them back in readiness for the following year's growth. The soil had been tilled, the fertiliser stock had been checked, and soon the bench grafting of the vines would begin. It was a never-ending cycle, and in the vats and fermentation tanks the new wines were maturing until they were ready to be marketed. When the bottled wines reached maturity they were sold privately, or through the Stellenbosch winery, and that involved a great deal of work.

Kate supervised the labelling of the bottles, and checked the orders due to be dispatched. At the loading base the estate truck was preparing to leave for the station, and when it finally drove away, its enormous tyres churning up the dust, everyone sighed with relief. That was it, but only until the following day.

Tiredness drove Kate to bed earlier than usual that night. Her head barely touched the pillow when she was asleep, but she awoke with a start some time later to see Rhyno approaching the bed.

'What do you think you're doing?' she demanded in a croaky voice when she saw his hands untying the belt of his robe.

'I'm coming to bed, what else?'

His robe slid from his shoulders, and her breath locked in her throat at the sight of his nakedness. Muscles bulged and rippled beneath his evenly-tanned skin with every movement he made, and she felt her pulse drumming in her ears as she dragged her eyes away from all that male vitality encased in his body.

'For God's sake, Rhyno, haven't you punished me enough?' she choked out the words as she felt the bed give way beneath his weight. 'Must you prolong it?'

'Your sentence will last until the day we file for a divorce,' he replied harshly, and his hands reached for her before she could leap out of bed. He turned her on to her back, and forced her to meet his eyes. 'Didn't I tell you?' he asked mockingly.

Her body went rigid when she felt the heat of his thighs against her own through the flimsy material of her nightdress, and her jaw seemed to ache with the effort to control her rioting emotions as she hissed, 'You're an insufferable, disgusting beast, and I hate you!'

His eyes darkened, and the arms that held her tightened like a vice. 'You've insulted me enough times, Kate, and you're going to pay for every one of them separately.'

'You're the most sadistic and revolting man it's ever been my misfortune to meet!' she almost shouted at him, trying desperately to ignore the fact that the clean male smell of him was stirring her senses wildly. 'Don't you know that your touch nauseates me?' she could not prevent herself from adding fuel to the fire of his anger.

'Just for that I'll make you beg, Kate.'

'*Never!*'

'You will, you know,' he said against her lips. 'Before this night has ended you will beg me to make love to you.'

'I'd rather die first!' she cried, straining away from him physically and mentally as she felt her treacherous body respond to the sensual caress of his hands.

'We'll see about that,' he laughed shortly and, as if to illustrate the power he had over her, he slid the strap of her nightdress off her shoulder, and cupped her breast in his hand.

'Take your hands off me!' she snapped, struggling against him, but those probing, caressing fingers sent a shudder of emotion surging through her, and a moan of pleasure burst from her lips moments before his searing kiss drove all thought of resistance from her mind.

Her nightdress, the only barrier between them, was swiftly removed, and his hands, warm and rough against her smooth skin, aroused a fire deep within her that flowed and pounded through her until every nerve and sinew seemed to quiver with an aching need. She felt his heart beating heavily against her breasts; beating almost in unison with hers, but for some reason she suspected that he was holding back even while he seemed intent upon driving her mad with desire and the most exquisite torment.

'Oh, please, I . . . I can't take much more of this,' she heard herself muttering in a voice quite unlike her own, and his mouth abruptly ceased its intoxicating exploration of her breast.

'Are you begging me to make love to you, Kate?'

A part of her drugged mind registered the significance of his harshly murmured query, but she was beyond caring and, discarding the final fragment of her pride, she cried brokenly, 'Oh, God . . . yes . . . take me, please!'

His hand tightened momentarily on her hip, then he broke her restraining clasp about his neck and rolled away from her. He got up out of bed, and put on his robe, then he turned and said abruptly, 'Not this time.'

Bewildered and confused, Kate sat up in bed with a jerky movement, uncaring that the sheets had slid to her waist to reveal taut, pointed breasts which were pale and smooth where the strip of her bikini had prevented the sun from caressing her skin to a golden tan. 'Where are you—you going?' she questioned him in a husky, broken voice.

'I'm going to sleep in the dressing-room.'

Kate's bewilderment increased. 'But—but you can't—you can't just leave me like this!'

'Can't I?'

His mouth was twisted in a ruthless smile which should have told her that he intended doing exactly as he had said, but her aroused body, with every nerve and pulse throbbing with an aching need, refused to accept what he was saying, and she cried frantically, 'Rhyno, for the love of heaven!'

'Heaven has nothing to do with it, Kate. Only hell,' he said, leaning over her suddenly and raking her with eyes filled with such contempt that she instantly dragged the sheets up about her naked, shivering body. 'Even if I have to drive you to hell and back, you will eventually learn to think twice before you dish out those insults you're so fond of.'

A sob rose in her throat, but she choked it back as anger came to her rescue, and with her hands clenched tightly on the sheets in an effort not to strike him, she hissed, 'You're a fiend, and a——'.

'Careful, Kate,' he warned her mockingly, and when the dressing-room door closed behind him, she threw herself face down on to the pillows.

'Oh, God!' she groaned, trying to control the tremors that shook through her. Her heated body craved fulfilment, but there was none forthcoming, and she became acquainted with a private hell which she would not have wished on her worst enemy.

'Why?' she asked herself repeatedly. *Why* did he do this to her? What satisfaction was there in it for him to punish her in this manner? Was he asleep, or was he, too, lying awake? she wondered, staring hard at the dressing-room door in the darkness. He had a slab of concrete where his heart ought to be, she told herself eventually, and a wave of chilled anger finally washed over her, drowning out her emotions.

She lay awake for several hours before she fell asleep,

and she awoke the following morning to find a note
propped up against a jar of face cream on the dressing
table. Her heart knocked against her ribs, and regardless
of the fact that she was wearing nothing at all, she leapt
out of bed and snatched up the note, to see Rhyno's bold
handwriting leaping out at her. Typically, it did not start
in the conventional manner, but simply said:

*I have to go to Cape Town on business, and I won't be back
until late this evening. I hope you slept well. Rhyno.*

Kate's hands shook when she read the message. The
first part was acceptable, but the last sentence was like a
physical blow where it hurt most. *I hope you slept well.* He
could not have been crueller had he tried, and helpless
anger was her only antidote against the humiliation,
shame, and utter despair that gripped her.

'*Damn you!*' she cried hotly, crushing the note in her
hands and flinging it viciously into the basket beside the
dressing-table. 'I wish you in *hell*, Rhyno van der Bijl!'

Rage and pain mingled to bring tears to her eyes, but
she dashed them away with the back of her hand, and
stormed into the bathroom to shower and dress herself in
comfortable slacks and a warm sweater.

She tried to forget about the note she had received while
she worked in the study, but half way through the morning she knew that it was impossible to forget, or to delude
herself. There was more to Rhyno's note than she cared
to dwell on, but her thoughts could not be stunted. What
was the nature of his business in Cape Town? And where
was Barbara? Did she go with him?

Kate tried to tell herself that she was torturing herself
needlessly, but a few minutes later her hand strayed towards the telephone on the desk, and before she could
prevent herself from doing so she was dialling the number
of the boutique.

The voice that answered was feminine, but it was not

Barbara's, and Kate's suspicions were once again aroused, but she nevertheless asked, 'May I speak to Miss Owen, please?'

'I'm afraid she isn't in today,' the girl replied with a brightness that made Kate want to scream. 'She left early this morning for Cape Town, but she should be back tomorrow.'

'I see,' Kate said dully.

'Is there a message, perhaps?' the girl at the other end asked eagerly after a strained little silence had elapsed. 'Could I ask her to call you back?'

'That won't be necessary, thank you.'

'But——'

'I'll call again some other time,' Kate ended the conversation abruptly, and her palm was damp when she replaced the receiver on its cradle.

She was never quite sure afterwards how she managed to get through the rest of the morning, but somehow she did, and after lunch that day she instructed the faithful Lenny to take over her duties in the cellars. She drove in to town with only one purpose in mind; to speak to Naomi van der Bijl, and to find out exactly what there was between Rhyno and Barbara.

It was an exceptionally warm day, considering that it was midwinter, and when she arrived at Naomi's cottage she found her pottering about in the colourful garden with a wide-brimmed straw hat on her head.

'Kate!' Naomi exclaimed when she turned at the sound of the garden gate squeaking and, taking off her gardening gloves, she walked towards the tall, slender girl coming up the path. 'How lovely to see you, my dear,' she smiled, taking Kate's arm and ushering her into the cottage.

'I hope you don't mind my coming here uninvited?' Kate asked tentatively when they stood facing each other in the small but neatly furnished lounge.

'Don't be silly, child,' Naomi laughed lightly, taking off her straw hat and flinging it into a chair. 'Please don't ever feel you need an invitation to come here to my home.'

Kate glanced appreciatively about the room. 'Is this where you've lived all these years since . . .'

'Since I sold La Reine to your late father?' Naomi finished for her when Kate paused uncomfortably. 'Yes, this has been my home ever since.'

'You've created a very homely atmosphere.'

'Why, thank you, Kate.' Dark brown eyes, very much like Rhyno's, smiled warmly at Kate. 'Shall I make us a pot of tea?'

'That would be nice, thank you,' Kate replied sighing inwardly with relief at the thought that she would have time to gather her wits about her.

'Make yourself comfortable, my dear,' Naomi suggested. 'I shan't be long.'

Left alone, Kate glanced about her with detached interest until she saw the photograph on the low, old-fashioned cabinet against the north-facing wall, and she crossed the room to study it more closely. The aristocratic features were less severe, the chiselled mouth was curved in a faint smile, and those dark eyes gazed directly into hers without contempt, but it was unmistakably Rhyno, a much younger Rhyno, with his serious face devoid of those stern, often harsh lines. Kate's throat tightened with emotion, and she wished she could have known him then before life, and circumstances, had twisted him into the harsh man she knew.

A light step behind her finally made her turn, and she seated herself opposite Naomi while she poured their tea, but her eyes strayed back to the photograph on the cabinet and lingered there almost hungrily.

'That photograph was taken during Rhyno's second

year at university,' Naomi said quietly, following the direction of Kate's glance as she handed her her tea, and Kate lowered her eyes guiltily.

'Was he always so serious?'

'He was always a very determined and dedicated boy,' Naomi explained. 'He still is,' she added after a pause, her eyes seeking Kate's. 'He is also very loyal to the people he cares for.'

Kate swallowed down a mouthful of tea to steady herself, but she could not quite suppress that hint of cynicism in her voice when she asked, 'Was it always his ambition to regain possession of La Reine?'

'No,' Naomi shook her head. 'For many years he swore never to set foot on La Reine again. What we've lost must remain lost for ever, he used to say. One can never go back.'

'How fortuitous for him that he changed his mind,' Kate replied, and again there was that hint of cynicism in her voice.

Naomi frowned as she studied Kate's slender figure in the chair opposite hers. She saw the slight tremor in the hand that held the tea-cup, and the faint shadows beneath eyes that gazed directly into hers, but it was the tightness about that usually soft mouth that made her ask with noticeable concern, 'What's troubling you, Kate?'

The tremor in the hand that held the tea-cup increased, but Kate's gaze did not falter as she said abruptly, 'Barbara Owen.'

'They've known each other for many years,' Naomi informed her after a noticeable hesitation. 'They were at university together.'

Kate's eyes widened with a measure of surprise. 'I didn't know Barbara had been to university.'

'She discontinued her studies after her second year.'

'Why?'

Naomi looked away. 'I'm afraid I can't answer that.'

'Can't, or won't?' Kate persisted curiously.

'I can't tell you, Kate,' Naomi replied, and looked decidedly uncomfortable as she explained, 'Rhyno and Barbara took me into their confidence some years ago, and I'm not in a position to tell you what you want to know.'

'I see,' Kate murmured thoughtfully, a plan of action forming in her mind with the swiftness of a veld fire as she drained her cup and placed it on the tray. 'Well, thanks for the tea, but I have several things to do before I return home.'

'Kate . . .' Naomi's hand touched Kate's as they rose to their feet, and the eyes that met Kate's contained a troubled apology, 'I'm sorry.'

'So am I,' Kate replied seriously, and her chin was set with determination when she drove away from Naomi van der Bijl's cottage a few minutes later. She had hoped to find an answer to her problem, but, like her son, Naomi had shut that particular door in Kate's face, leaving Kate no alternative but to seek help elsewhere in her effort to find out what she wanted to know.

'This is a pleasant surprise, Kate,' Hubert Walton smiled at her from across the room half an hour later when she was ushered into his office. 'Do you realise that it's months since I last had the pleasure of your company?'

'Since when have you needed an invitation to come out to Solitaire?' Kate counter-questioned as she seated herself in front of his desk.

'I plead guilty, but I've been rather busy lately,' Hubert told her ruefully as he leaned back in his chair and studied her thoughtfully. 'What can I do for you?'

'Do you know of someone in Cape Town who could dig up some information for you?' Kate asked without hesitation, her hands tightening on the clasp of her handbag.

'What kind of information?'

For a moment only the sound of the traffic in the street below filled the room, then Kate said: 'Barbara Owen went to university more or less at the same time as Rhyno. There must be someone, one or two of her acquaintances, perhaps, who could give us more detailed information about her.'

'I repeat, Kate, what kind of information?'

'I believe she dropped out of university after her second year, and I want to know why.'

'Why don't you ask Rhyno, he should know.'

'He refuses to discuss Barbara with me.'

Hubert observed her for a moment in speculative silence, then he pressed the tips of his fingers neatly together, and demanded quietly, 'Why is this of such importance to you?'

'I don't know yet,' Kate shrugged slightly. 'I'll know when I get the information I'm looking for.'

Hubert studied her with a look of deep concentration on his lined face, and Kate was beginning to think that he would refuse when he finally sighed and said: 'I'll do my best for you, Kate, but I can't promise you anything.'

'That's fine . . . but there's one other thing,' Kate said when he followed her example and rose to his feet. 'I don't want Rhyno to know about this.'

His glance sharpened beneath those grey, bushy eyebrows, then he nodded abruptly. 'If that's what you want.'

'Thanks, Uncle Hubert,' she smiled, inwardly relieved, then she kissed him impulsively on the cheek and walked out of his office.

She drove back to Solitaire that afternoon feeling intensely satisfied, but as the hours passed her satisfaction turned to apprehension. What would she discover that she did not know already? What was there between Rhyno and Barbara that was so confidential that Naomi felt herself sworn to silence? Frightening thoughts darted back and forth through her mind, but she was determined not to leap to conclusions until she was totally aware of the facts.

She had dinner alone that evening and went to bed early, but found that she could not sleep. Her ears were straining for the sound of Rhyno's car and, regardless of her efforts, she was awake several hours later when she heard his Citroën approaching the house. She waited, following his movements in her mind, and her body tensed when she eventually heard his footsteps in the passage outside her door. Her heart leapt uncomfortably when she heard him pause, then his footsteps continued on into the dressing-room. She eventually heard him whistling softly and tunelessly in the shower across the passage, and the whistling continued until she heard him re-enter the dressing-room.

She rolled over on to her left side, lying with her back towards the door to give the impression that she was asleep if he should enter her room, but her body was tense and, no matter how much she tried, every nerve seemed to be quivering expectantly. The memory of the previous night was still too fresh and raw in her memory, and although she dreaded the thought, a part of her willed him to come to her. She despised herself for it, but when at last the dressing-room door opened and closed quietly, she could not deny that she was aware of his presence in the room with every fibre of her being. She tried desperately to control her breathing, to give the impression that she was asleep, but her heart was pounding so hard and fast in her breast that she was almost convinced that he could hear it. She felt the springs sag beneath his weight when he got into bed beside her, then his hand was beneath her nightdress, and sliding up her warm, silken thigh until his fingers tightened on her hip.

'Kate . . .'

She ignored him mentally, but physically she responded to that fiery touch, and she trembled despite herself, giving him a clear indication that she was awake and acutely conscious of his lean, muscular frame beside her in that enormous bed. In one swift movement she was turned over on to her back and trapped against him.

'For pity's sake, Rhyno, leave me in peace,' she groaned, realising the futility of pretence as she tried to avoid his seeking lips, but they trailed a fiery path of destruction across her shoulder, and shivers of delight rippled through her when she felt his teeth nipping softly at her ear.

'You don't really want me to leave you alone, do you?'

'Yes, I do,' she insisted, her hands against his shoulders, and the muscles in her arms aching as she vainly tried to thrust him from her.

'Why?'

'Do I have to spell it out for you?' she demanded angrily, her senses responding to the scent of his masculine cologne, and the tantalising caress of his lips against her exposed throat, but before he could reply she said accusingly, 'You were with Barbara today.'

'So what?' he demanded in a voice ringing with hateful arrogance.

'Haven't you had enough sex for one day?'

'So you imagine I'm some sort of sex maniac?'

He was laughing at her, she could sense it, and added to that there was the memory of how he had abandoned her the previous night. Everything within her suddenly leapt into revolt, and her voice shook with fury as she snapped, 'Oh, for heaven's sake, Rhyno, I couldn't care less about your sexual appetite, but I'm not in the mood to be used as the object of your sadistic pleasure, so just leave me alone!'

'Kate the shrew,' he muttered harshly, his arms tightening about her slim body. 'I shall enjoy taming you, and when I've succeeded you'll find I shall be the one to call the tune.'

'I'll see you in hell first!' she cried furiously, fighting off his hands when he began to strip off her nightdress, but her efforts were futile.

She fought like a wildcat, determined not to give in for fear of a repetition of the night before, but she had no defence against the waves of sensual pleasure that swept through her, and she despised herself as she found herself yielding to the urgent intimacy of his caresses until there was no room for thought in her mind.

Rhyno did not leave her this time, and her need rose to meet his until their bodies became fused together in the throes of a fierce passion. Caught in the grip of the most intense, soul-shattering pleasure, everything else was forgotten, and she clung to him in helpless surrender, not caring what he might think of her, but knowing that she would be ashamed of herself later for her lack of control.

Kate did not realise it at first, but that night was the start of a changing pattern in their lives. Instead of attacking, she was on the defensive, instead of dishing out insults she was the one who was being insulted and humiliated, and knowing the reason for it did not help her to accept it. She loved Rhyno with every breath she took, but she would rather have died than place this final weapon of destruction in his hands.

CHAPTER NINE

THREE weeks after paying a visit to Hubert Walton's offices, Kate received a message that he would like her to come and see him as soon as possible, and she wasted no time in making an appointment for that same day.

Finding an acceptable excuse for driving in to town that afternoon was no problem, but apprehension was knotting her stomach when she walked into the attorney's office and seated herself. He smiled at her across the wide expanse of his desk, and for a few minutes they discussed everything from the weather to Aunt Edwina's visit to Cape Town. His obvious reluctance to get to the point awakened a gnawing fear, and Hubert Walton, knowing that he could no longer prolong the inevitable, shuffled the papers before him, and faced her grimly.

'I have some information here which might interest you, but I don't think you're going to like it.'

'Whether I like it or not is of no consequence.' Her throat felt dry, but her palms were cold and damp as she leaned forward in her chair. 'I must know, Uncle Hubert.'

The attorney cleared his throat characteristically, and lowered his gaze. 'You were right about Rhyno and Barbara Owen being at university together. According to the information I received it was generally assumed that she was Rhyno's girl-friend.'

'Is that all?' Kate asked stiffly when a few seconds elapsed with only the hum of the air-conditioner filling the room.

'Are you sure you want me to go on?' Hubert asked

hesitantly, a frown between his bushy eyebrows.

'Don't keep me in suspense,' she replied with a hint of sarcasm in her voice which was directed at no one in particular, and Hubert fiddled with his papers once more before he continued.

'Rhyno was in his final year at varsity and Barbara in her second year when she became pregnant and was forced to relinquish her studies.'

Shock, like a vicious blow in her midriff, robbed her momentarily of breath, and her hands unconsciously tightened on the arms of the chair. 'Was Rhyno the father of her child?'

'So everyone believed.'

Kate's mind was in a frantic turmoil, she couldn't think straight, and logic was something that deserted her completely at that moment. Fact and supposition mingled to form a horrifying picture that made her feel sick inside.

'Why didn't he marry her?' she questioned Hubert in a voice that sounded as cold as she felt.

'I'm afraid I can't answer that,' he shrugged.

'What happened to the child?'

'She's living with Barbara's parents in Cape Town.'

'Do you have their address?'

'Yes, it's in Rondebosch, if I'm not mistaken.' He found the address among his papers, scribbled it on to a slip of paper, and handed it to her with an anxious query in his eyes. 'You're not thinking of going there, are you?'

'No, but . . .' She hesitated, not quite sure yet what she wanted to do with the address he had given her, but she folded it between her trembling fingers and slipped it into her handbag. 'I might need the address some time in the future, one never knows,' she said at length, closing her handbag and raising her glance to his.

Hubert Walton looked uncomfortable and genuinely distressed. He had known Kate since the day that she was born, and nothing could have pained him more than to pass this information on to her. She was pale but composed as she sat there facing him, and he could not help but admire her.

'Kate, I'm——'

'Was there anything else?' she interrupted him quickly, sensing his discomfort.

'No,' he shook his head.

'Thanks for your help,' she said with forced brightness, getting unsteadily to her feet and extending her hand towards him.

His fingers tightened about hers. 'Don't thank me. I'm only sorry that I——' He paused abruptly and, releasing her hand, he gestured vaguely. 'You know what I mean.'

'I know what you mean,' Kate whispered, then she turned quickly and walked out of his office before those despicable tears spilled from her eyes.

She had driven a few kilometres out of town before she parked her Mercedes off the road and gave way to the tears which were blurring her vision. It was all very well suspecting something, but learning the truth was quite a different matter.

Was it the truth?

She wiped her eyes and blew her nose. That question had blasted its way into her mind, bringing with it that much-needed thread of logic, and while the late afternoon sun dipped towards the west, bathing the valley in a golden hue, Kate stared straight ahead of her with unseeing eyes while she tried to unravel the information she had received. Some of it was fact, and some of it was pure speculation, but it was difficult trying to decide on the reliability of the latter.

If Rhyno was the father of Barbara's child, then why had he not married her? It hurt like the very devil to think of it, but she had to; she had to try and make some sense out of this whole shocking business. She could some-how not imagine that Rhyno would have shirked his res-ponsibilities to this extent, and yet Barbara had merely to call for him to hasten to her side.

She sighed and started the car. She was too puzzled and confused to think rationally at that moment. Perhaps tomorrow she would see it all in a different light when the pain was not so intense with every thought that flitted through her mind.

At the dinner table that evening Kate found herself studying Rhyno when she thought he was not looking, and instinct suddenly told her that he could not be the father of Barbara's child. She could not explain to herself afterwards why she felt so strongly about this, but she knew, and after that the hurt was not so intense. At the same time she also realised that she actually knew very little about the man she had married under such im-possible circumstances, but she was determined that this was something which she would rectify as soon as pos-sible.

'You've been staring at me all evening as if you've never seen me before,' Rhyno startled her with his observation when he got into bed beside her that evening.

'Perhaps I'm seeing you for the first time as you really are,' she parried his remark with that usual hint of sarcasm in her voice as a defence against the truth.

Rhyno stared hard at her and, when she would have turned her face away to avoid his intense scrutiny, his fingers trapped her chin, forcing her to meet his eyes. 'What exactly do you mean by that?'

'I don't really know you very well, do I?' she explained lamely, her lashes veiling the expression in her eyes. 'We married each other to claim our inheritance, and for some weeks now you've been sharing my bed, but I still know very little about you.'

The pressure of his fingers lightened into a caress that made her pulse quicken, but his hard mouth curved with derisive mockery. 'You know all the important things, and the rest is none of your business.'

'Does Barbara have some sort of hold over you?' she questioned daringly, and the next instant his harsh laugh jarred her sensitive nerves.

'No woman will ever have a hold over me,' he told her bluntly, his fingers biting briefly into her shoulders before his hand slid down her body to mould her hips to his. 'Not even you, Kate.'

His mouth descended to silence her barbed reply, and then she was lost. She had realised some time ago that it was senseless to fight against the pleasure only he could give her, and she surrendered herself willingly to the intoxication of his lean, demanding body, but, as always, she held back subconsciously, not giving of herself entirely.

Kate drove across to La Reine a few days later, but she could not imagine what she hoped to find there. In all the years it had belonged to her father, she had entered the homestead only once, to deliver a message to the previous estate manager, but now, as she stared at the silent, gabled house, she felt the urge to enter again what had once been Rhyno's home.

She parked her car beside the honeysuckle hedge and approached the house hesitantly. It was all very well wanting to go inside, but how was she going to do that without a key? Rhyno would keep it locked, she was certain of that, yet when her hand touched the heavy brass handle on the front door it opened beneath her touch. Surprised, and more than a little concerned, she stepped into the hall where the stained glass windows above the door cast patterns on the yellow-wood floor. The house was obviously being cleaned and aired regularly, but it was ominously silent as she wandered through the vast rooms which were sparsely furnished with bits and pieces from Solitaire. Her eyes searched for something belonging to Rhyno; something which might give her an indication as to what kind of man he was, but there was nothing except a few farming magazines in what was once the study. A few battered books had been stacked up in the shelves against the wall behind the desk, and one in particular caught her eye. It was a volume of poetry, and she she removed it carefully, blowing the layer of dust off its cover before she examined it more closely.

She paged through it slowly, recognising some of her old favourites, and for a while she had no conception of time or place until a photograph slid from its hiding place between those yellowed pages. It was a photograph of a much younger Barbara sandwiched between a youthful-looking Rhyno and a fair-haired young man who not only looked handsome, but obviously knew it too. Kate's hand shook as she replaced the photograph, and only then did she notice the two lines of a poem which had been heavily underlined.

Hard is her heart as flint or stone,
She laughs to see me pale.

Did those words refer to Barbara? Surely not, Kate thought. Barbara was not like that at all. But who else? Those underlined sentences reflected the heart of a man who loved, and a stab of jealousy and pain tore at her insides.

'Were you looking for something?'

The book snapped shut between Kate's nervous fingers, and her heart leapt into her throat as she swung round to face the man who had entered the room so quietly. Her eyes were fixed on those harsh features, seeking vainly for a softening which was never there for her, and then, with a heart that was pounding heavily, she said lamely, 'I . . . the front door was open . . .'

'It was unlocked, but it was not open,' he corrected blandly, then a cynical smile curved his mouth. 'What did you hope to find, Kate?'

'Nothing, I——' She swallowed nervously and averted her eyes. 'I'd only been here once before, and I—I was curious.'

'Have you satisfied your curiosity?' Rhyno asked abruptly, removing the book from her nerveless fingers and returning it to the shelf.

Kate stared at his broad back in the blue checked shirt which seemed to be almost a size too small, and fought against the ache in her throat before she answered his question with a query of her own. 'Why are you treating me like a trespasser?'

'You *are* trespassing, Kate,' he stated bluntly, and turned in time to witness her cheeks reddening with humiliation.

'You don't consider that you're doing the same at Solitaire?' she hit back.

'I'm carrying out, to the letter, the instructions in your father's will.'

Anger brought an edge to her voice. 'I don't recall anything in my father's will which gave you access to my body.'

'You brought that on yourself when you disregarded our agreement.' His eyes mocked her ruthlessly. 'You must admit, though, that it's a delightful way of passing the time.'

'You filthy swine!' she spat out the words furiously, only to retreat the next instant when he advanced towards her purposefully.

'Shall I prove to you here and now how much you've enjoyed these past weeks?'

'If you touched me now I'd be physically ill,' she cried hoarsely, and fled from him, her eyes blinded by tears as she sped out of the house to where she had parked her car.

She grated the gears, reversed wildly, then drove away at a speed that made the car sway and bump crazily across the uneven track. She did not look back, but she had a feeling that Rhyno was watching her, and her foot went down automatically. The Mercedes leapt forward with a renewed burst of energy as if the devil himself were on its tail, but it skidded on the loose sand, and only by some miracle did Kate maintain control of the vehicle as it spun round and finally came to a halt in a cloud of dust with its nose facing the way she had come.

Distraught and shocked, she put her head down on to the steering wheel and wept a little hysterically. This type of irrational behaviour was quite unlike her, and she admonished herself severely when she finally regained control of herself. It was senseless allowing Rhyno to affect her in this way, but—oh, God, how did she cope with the knowledge that she had given her love where it was not wanted?

For the next few days Kate could think of nothing else but those underlined words of the poem. *Hard is her heart as flint or stone, she laughs to see me pale*. What did it mean? And why was the place marked with a photograph in which Barbara Owen appeared? There was so much to think about; so much that puzzled her, but she came no closer to finding an explanation for it all.

She was on her way to the breakfast-room early one morning when the telephone rang in the hall, and when she lifted the receiver it was Barbara's voice that said: 'Kate, I apologise for telephoning at this unearthly hour of the morning, but I must speak to Rhyno urgently.'

'I'll call him,' Kate answered her abruptly and, placing

the receiver on the table, she crossed the hall and walked down the passage to their bedroom. Rhyno emerged from the bathroom, fully dressed, and she gave him no more than a cursory glance as she said stiffly, 'It's Barbara on the phone. She wants to speak to you urgently.'

She followed him from the room, but in the hall she turned off to the left to wait for him in the breakfast-room. His muted voice reached her ears, but she could not hear what he was saying, and as she stared at the bacon and eggs before her she promptly lost her appetite. What were they talking about, and what new scheme were they hatching to spend some time together?

Rhyno walked into the breakfast-room a few minutes later and helped himself to the omelette which he preferred, and a slice of toast. Kate watched him eat in silence, marvelling at his calm, unperturbed manner, and she hovered on the brink of questioning him about the call he had received from Barbara, but somehow she remained silent.

'I'll be leaving for Cape Town just as soon as I've had breakfast,' he informed her almost as if he had sensed her curiosity.

'Is that where Barbara telephoned from?'

'Yes.'

Kate wrung the table napkin between her hands without actually knowing what she was doing. 'I suppose you can't tell me what it is that makes you run to her aid the minute she calls?'

He looked up sharply, and his expression was grim as his eyes pinned her to her chair. 'I told you before, you wouldn't understand.'

'Try me.'

'I haven't the time or the inclination, Kate,' he brushed aside her suggestion with hurtful impatience.

'Now, if you'll pour me a cup of coffee, I can be on my way in a few minutes.'

Perilously close to tears, but determined not to show it, she poured his coffee and passed it to him. If only he would confide in her, she thought despairingly, but it seemed as though she was wishing for the impossible. Perhaps if she confronted him with what she knew it might help to bring it all out into the open, she decided, and when Rhyno pushed back his chair and rose to his feet, she followed his example.

'Rhyno?' she said hesitantly, not quite knowing how to begin.

'I'm in a hurry, Kate. What is it?'

She raised her hands in an appealing gesture, but his expression remained shuttered and unrelenting. She knew that it would be impossible to reach him, and her hands fell helplessly to her sides as she muttered lamely, 'Nothing.'

Rhyno gave her a withering look before he strode out of the room, and a few minutes later he was driving away from Solitaire to keep his appointment with Barbara.

During the winter months Kate nearly always spent her mornings in the study, catching up on the pile of paperwork, but this morning she could not concentrate on what she was doing. Her mind was elsewhere . . . in Rondebosch . . . and after an hour of indecision, she acted on an impulse and almost ran into her bedroom to find that address Hubert Walton had given her. It was time this distasteful situation was brought out into the open, and she knew now that there was only one way to do it. No matter how much it might hurt, she had to find out the truth behind these frequent and secretive meetings.

Half an hour after making this decision, she was speeding towards Cape Town. She had no idea, as yet, what she was going to say, or do for that matter, but whatever happened she had to know the truth.

It was midday before she arrived in Cape Town, and then she had some difficulty in locating the Owen house in Rondebosch, but when at last she parked her car in the street outside their spacious home she was taut with nerves. Rhyno's car was parked in the driveway, and so was Barbara's. On the lawn, beneath a shady tree, a fair-haired little girl of six or seven was playing with her dolls, and she looked up curiously when Kate pushed open the gate and closed it carefully behind her.

'Hello,' Kate smiled at her tentatively. 'What's your name?'

'Stephanie,' the child lisped without hesitation, leaving her dolls for a moment to inspect Kate more closely.

'Is your mummy at home?' Kate asked unnecessarily.

A chubby forefinger pointed in the direction of the house. 'She's in there.'

Kate thanked her and walked up the path towards the front door, but her movements were jerky, and her heart was beating so hard and fast that it almost choked her. What if she had made a mistake by coming here? What if it only made matters worse? What if . . .?

The front door stood open, and from inside the murmur of voices reached her ears. Her finger hovered on the bell button, but she changed her mind. The element of surprise would perhaps have the best effect, she decided as she stepped inside, and her footsteps were muted on the thick pile of the carpet as she crossed the hall and walked towards what was obviously the living-room.

She paused in the doorway, and her insides jerked violently, leaving her with a sick feeling at the pit of her stomach. Rhyno stood in the centre of the modernly furnished room with his back towards the door, and Barbara was in his arms with her head pressed into his shoulder. She was murmuring something to which Rhyno grunted his obvious approval, then she raised her head, and Kate had the satisfaction of seeing her face pale considerably when their eyes met over Rhyno's shoulder.

'Kate!' she exclaimed, and her voice sounded a pitch higher than usual when Rhyno released her abruptly and swung round to face the door. He looked a little pale beneath his tan, but it could have been Kate's imagination, for there was unmistakable anger in the taut line of his jaw, and the burning intensity of his eyes sent a little shudder of fear coursing through her. There was an awkward, tense silence which seemed to last for ages, then Barbara said unsteadily, 'We didn't expect you.'

'I realise that,' Kate replied quietly, a strange calmness taking possession of her, but deep down inside of her there was an ache that nothing could assuage at that moment.

Barbara's glance darted swiftly in Rhyno's direction before settling once more on Kate. 'I know what you must be thinking, but——'

'At the moment I'm not thinking anything except that it's time the three of us sat down and had a serious discussion,' Kate interrupted her.

'The discussion can wait,' Rhyno spoke for the first time, and his voice sounded harsh and angry as he added: 'Barbara has enough problems at the moment without you adding to them.'

Kate flinched inwardly at his obvious determination to shut her out, but Barbara intervened. 'Kate is right,' she said. 'It *is* time we talked this thing out.'

'Barbara!' he warned, but she silenced him with a gesture of her hand, and drew Kate further into the room.

'You should have taken Kate into your confidence months ago, Rhyno,' Barbara reproached him.

'Possibly, but before anything else is said there are a few questions I would like to ask.' Rhyno's expression was granite-hard as he turned to face Kate, and she felt her insides quiver with apprehension. 'Who gave you this address?' he demanded bitingly.

'You're not the only one who can carry out a successful investigation, you know,' Kate replied at once, relying heavily on sarcasm in order to hide her incredible nervousness and misery.

'Did my mother tell you?' he shot the next question at her.

'No,' Kate shook her head and forced herself to endure his angry surveillance. 'I hired someone to get the information I wanted.'

Rhyno's eyebrows rose sharply. 'You know about Stephanie?'

'I've known about her for more than a week now,' Kate confessed with a calmness which belied the turmoil within her.

'And you never said anything?' Rhyno persisted relentlessly.

Kate shrugged helplessly, lowering her lashes to hide the pain mirrored in her eyes. 'I was hoping you would tell me voluntarily.'

There was no sign of remorse on his hard face, only a cynical twisting of his mouth. 'I hope you were satisfied with the information you received?'

'The only fact I'm in possession of is that Barbara had to relinquish her studies when she became pregnant,' Kate replied with rising resentment, then she gestured vaguely with her cold hands. 'The rest is pure supposition.'

'You've drawn your own conclusions, no doubt.'

Kate stared at him for a moment, aware of Barbara observing her with an equal intensity, and a feeling of intense isolation made her shiver involuntarily as she said: 'I have.'

There was a brief, strained silence which was disturbed only by the ticking of the clock on the mantelshelf, and the heavy, painful thudding of Kate's heart, then Barbara stepped forward and gripped Kate's hands with her own.

'Kate . . .' she began, and the note of anxiety in her voice was unmistakable. 'Rhyno isn't the father of my child.'

'I know.' Kate swallowed convulsively, and ventured a quick glance in Rhyno's direction to glimpse his frowning disapproval. 'Whatever else he may be, he would never shirk his responsibilities.'

A profound silence followed her disclosure. She had spoken the truth, straight from the heart, and for some reason she had left them stunned.

Barbara was the first to recover. She tightened her grip on Kate's hands, and glanced at Rhyno to state triumphantly, 'I told you she would understand, didn't I?'

'So you did,' Rhyno acknowledged, the expression in his dark eyes unfathomable when they met Kate's.

'Please sit down, Kate. I'd like to explain why I needed to consult Rhyno so urgently.' Barbara ushered Kate towards the sofa and sat down next to her, but Rhyno turned towards the fireplace and lit his pipe in that methodical manner Kate knew so well while Barbara proceeded to explain. 'My parents have looked after Stephanie all these years, but they're not as young as they used to be, and they're finding it difficult to cope with a small child in the house. I've never been much good at making decisions on my own, and I'm afraid I've always leaned rather heavily on Rhyno in the past.' Her smile was tinged with guilt as she added: 'That's why he's here.'

Relief, perhaps, made it all sound so extraordinarily uncomplicated, and when Kate thought of that lovely child playing outside in the garden, her compassionate heart drove her to say reprovingly, 'You're not thinking of putting Stephanie into some sort of home, are you?'

Barbara lowered her eyes with an embarrassed laugh.

'Can you imagine what people will say in Stellenbosch when they discover that I'm an unmarried mother?'

'The tongues may wag for a while, but they'll soon find something else to talk about,' Kate brushed aside her remark. 'If you want Stephanie with you, then there's really nothing to stop you from taking her back to Stellenbosch with you. The important thing is your happiness, and the child's.'

'That's what Rhyno has been telling me, but——'

'Then why don't you take his advice, and we'll back you up all the way?' Kate suggested, her eyes meeting Rhyno's across the room. She searched for something; approval perhaps, or some sign of softening, but his rock-like features conveyed nothing on which her hungry heart could feed, and then Barbara was hugging her profusely, drawing her attention away from Rhyno.

'Oh, Kate, you're wonderful!' she seemed to be crying and laughing simultaneously. 'I feel much happier now that you know everything, and I'm going to take your advice. To hell with what people might say. From now on *I'm* going to take charge of my daughter.'

Kate's smile was a little wary when Barbara finally released her. She felt unsure of herself, and not quite certain what she ought to do. Rhyno had not moved from his stance beside the fireplace, and when her eyes sought his she caught a fleeting glimpse of something that made her heart leap wildly in her breast, but it was gone so quickly that she could only think she must have imagined it.

Barbara's parents arrived at the house just as Kate was about to leave, and they made it totally impossible for her to refuse their invitation to stay to lunch. Their presence eased whatever tensions might have arisen, and Kate found herself accepted on the strength of their long-standing friendship with Rhyno.

Throughout lunch Kate could not help but notice the change in Rhyno. He seemed relaxed in the company of Barbara and her parents, and his rare smiles appeared more frequently. It filled Kate with an aching longing to see him smile at her just once, but whenever their eyes met across the table his expression became coldly detached. She had intruded into something from which Rhyno had wanted to exclude her, and she began to suspect that this was what he was trying to convey to her. She was an intruder, an obnoxious weed in a bed of silky-petalled poppies, and the sooner she left, the better.

She took her leave of everyone immediately after lunch. Barbara begged her to stay a while longer, but she refused and, to her surprise, Rhyno accompanied her out to her car. The silence between them was awkward and uncomfortable. She wanted to say something, *anything* to relieve this terrible tension, but her heart felt heavy, and her mind remained a frightening blank.

'I'll be following you in a few minutes,' he said when she slid behind the wheel of her Mercedes.

She tried to speak, but her throat felt too dry, and she simply nodded her head abruptly as she stared up at him. His eyes were shuttered, but it seemed as if he was about to say something else, then he changed his mind and closed the door firmly, shutting out the cold breeze which had sprung up from a south-easterly direction.

The engine purred to life beneath her trembling fingers, and as she drove away she glanced into the rear-view mirror. Rhyno was no longer standing where she had left him, and his absence seemed to fill her with a biting desolation.

On the way back to Solitaire she debated her actions that day. It had perhaps been wrong of her to burst in on them the way she had done, but now, at least, she knew the truth . . . or *most* of it. Several questions still pounded through her mind, but they would have to remain un-answered. She had intruded far enough, and she dared not intrude further until she was certain of where she stood.

The weather changed abruptly from mild to cold. Clouds gathered in the sky, and when Kate arrived at Solitaire that afternoon it looked as though they could expect rain. She changed quickly into denims, a warm sweater, and her leather jacket, and she was on her way to the cellars when Rhyno's Citroën came up the circular drive.

Her heart skipped an uncomfortable beat at the sight of him, but she did not pause in her stride. It was only when he called her name that she stopped and turned to see him walking towards her. What now? she wondered, her eyes on his stern features. Was she going to be berated for intruding where she had not been wanted?

His hand brushed against hers when he fell into step beside her, and that light, impersonal touch activated a thousand little nerves, but it was nothing in comparison to what she felt when he said evenly, 'Thank you for being so understanding.'

Her steps faltered and stopped. She turned to face him, and had to look a long way up to meet his eyes.

'Did it surprise you to learn that my mind is not as twisted as you imagined?' she flung one of his earlier in-sults back at him, and his eyes darkened with anger.

'Dammit, Kate, I——'

'There's one question I would like to ask, and if you don't want to answer it, then we'll leave it at that,' she interrupted him boldly now that her confidence in herself had been restored. 'What happened to the father of Barbara's child? Why didn't she marry him?'

'He was already married,' Rhyno told her bluntly after a momentary hesitation. 'He was a very close friend of mine, but not even I knew that he had a wife until Barbara confronted him with the news that she was expecting his child.'

'I see,' Kate murmured, understanding a great deal more than before. 'So you allowed everyone to think that you were the father?'

'It didn't matter to me what people thought,' he replied harshly. 'I felt responsible for the mess she'd landed herself in.'

'Why?'

His expression became grim. 'I introduced them to each other.'

'And that made you feel guilty?'

'Does that surprise you?'

'I never credited you with such sensitivity,' she replied sharply, lowering her eyes before the mockery in his, then she shrugged and turned away. 'If you'll excuse me, I have work to do.'

'There's something else you ought to know.' His fingers snaked about her wrist, preventing her from leaving, and her pulse throbbed beneath those strong fingers. 'I asked Barbara to marry me at the time, but she refused.'

Kate was too stunned to reply, and it took her a few seconds to pull herself together mentally before she could speak. 'I think I would have done the same,' she said stiffly, twisting her wrist free of his clasp. 'No woman wants to be married for any other reason except love.'

Rhyno could have reminded her that love had had nothing to do with their reasons for marrying each other, but he didn't. He merely thrust his clenched fists into the pockets of his pants, and cast a frowning glance across the vineyards as he said: 'Marrying me would have saved her quite a number of problems.'

'It would also have made you both thoroughly miserable,' she countered logically.

'I doubt it.' He turned to look at her, but she had a horrible feeling that he did not actually see her, and that hurt more than anything else. 'I have a lot of work to catch up on,' he changed the subject.

'So have I,' she said tritely, and they parted company, going in opposite directions.

They were always going in opposite directions in every possible way, and she resisted the temptation to look back at him when she felt those ridiculous tears in her eyes which seemed to come so easily these days.

CHAPTER TEN

KATE's life changed drastically during the following two weeks. The relationship between Rhyno and herself was strained, but he did not exclude her from his efforts to ease the way for Barbara when she arrived in Stellenbosch with Stephanie and, surprisingly, the child's presence caused no more than a minor upheaval in the community. Aunt Edwina also returned during this time from her visit to Cape Town, and she arrived at Solitaire with more vigour than when she had departed. It was good to have her back, and her presence somehow eased a great deal of the tension in the house.

The third, and most distressing thing that happened during this time was the fact that Kate was beginning to suffer from slight bouts of nausea. It disturbed her only vaguely at first, but it eventually filled her with grave concern.

'You haven't eaten a thing, Kate,' Aunt Edwina complained one morning at the breakfast table when Kate pushed her plate aside and helped herself to a cup of coffee.

'I'm not hungry.'

Edwina Duval eyed her niece critically. 'Have you been to see a doctor?'

'For goodness' sake, Aunt Edwina,' Kate laughed uneasily, 'I'm not ill, and I'm simply not hungry.'

'It wouldn't do any harm to see a doctor.'

That awful suspicion leapt into Kate's mind once again, but she thrust it aside forcibly, and smiled at her aunt. 'If it would set your mind at rest, then I might just do that.'

'Why don't you ring him now and make an appointment?'

'I'm in no hurry,' Kate shrugged, shrinking inwardly from the mere idea of having to see a doctor, but her aunt was in no mood to be crossed.

'Kate!' she said in that authoritative tone which Kate knew so well. It meant, 'Do it now, or I'll do it for you.'

'Oh, very well!' Kate sighed, and with a great deal of reluctance and trepidation she left the breakfast-room to telephone the doctor's consulting-rooms and make an appointment.

That afternoon, while she sat leafing idly through a magazine in the doctor's waiting-room, she tried to convince herself that her problem was nothing more than a digestive upset, but when she emerged from the consulting-room half an hour later her worst suspicions had been confirmed. She had felt tempted to shout, 'It can't be! It's impossible!' And yet, when she thought about it, she had done absolutely nothing to prevent something like this happening. The signs had been there, but she had ignored them while so many other problems had taken priority in her mind.

She could no longer evade the truth, or thrust it from her. She had to face facts. She was going to have Rhyno's child, and she dared not let him know it. She had become acquainted with his deep sense of responsibility, and it was not difficult to guess what he would do, but continuing with their marriage for the sake of the child was an abhorrent thought.

She sat in her car, hovering somewhere between hysterical laughter and choking tears, but she surrendered to neither, and drove instead to Hubert Walton's offices. He was the only one she could turn to with this new problem, and she clung to the desperate hope that he could help her.

'Come in, Kate, and sit down,' Hubert said some fifteen minutes later, then his glance sharpened, and he stared hard at the girl approaching his desk. 'You don't look too well, if you'll forgive me saying so.'

'I'm fine,' she lied grimly. 'Just fine.'

'What can I do for you this afternoon?' he asked the moment she was seated, his eyes dwelling on her pale, pinched face.

'Would it affect my inheritance in any way if I went away for the remaining months of my marriage?'

'I'm afraid it would, Kate,' he frowned. 'Why do you ask?'

'It—It's important, that's all,' she stammered help-lessly, reluctant to tell him the truth. 'I *must* go away.'

'But why, Kate?' Hubert insisted. 'If you explain your reasons for wanting to go away then I might still be able to help you in some way.'

Restlessness and a certain amount of anxiety drove her to her feet, and she crossed the room to stand staring out of the window at the slow-moving traffic in the street below. She could not face this man who knew her almost as well as her own family, but she knew that she owed him the truth and, staring fixedly at nothing in particular, she said bluntly, 'I'm pregnant.'

She sensed his surprise in the brief silence that followed, then he said hesitantly, 'So your marriage——'

'Is a real one,' she filled in for him when he paused awkwardly. She turned then to face him, and her eyes were wide and pleading in her white, strained face. 'You've *got* to help me, Uncle Hubert!'

'I'm afraid I don't understand.' He shook his head as if to emphasise this fact. 'Perhaps you should sit down again, my dear, and tell me why it's so important for you to go away.'

She obeyed with a sigh, and clasped her hands tightly

in her lap. 'I don't want Rhyno to know that I'm going to have his child.'

'But why not, for heaven's sake?' Hubert Walton demanded with incredulity mirrored in his eyes.

'For the simple reason that I don't want him to feel obliged to continue with our marriage when this year is up.'

'But if your marriage has progressed this far——'

'He doesn't love me,' she interrupted chokingly, and the attorney was clearly taken aback.

'Are you sure of that?' he demanded at length with a deep frown settling between his heavy brows.

'I'm positive.'

'And you, Kate? How do you feel about him?'

She stared at him across the desk, and her face went a shade paler. Her own feelings were too painfully raw as yet to discuss with anyone and, lowering her gaze to her tightly clenched hands, she said unsteadily, 'My feelings don't matter in this instance.'

'Kate . . .' Hubert got up and walked round his desk. He pulled up a chair close to hers, and sat down, then he took one of her clenched hands in his, and uncurled the finger gently. His touch was fatherly and comforting, but there was no comfort in his words when he spoke. 'I can't alter the wording of your father's will, my dear. I can only suggest that you and Rhyno sort this problem out between yourselves.'

'But I *can't* tell him I'm going to have his child!' she protested, her voice hoarse with anxiety and fear. 'I know what he'll do. He'll insist on continuing with our marriage, and I'd rather die than have him stay with me for that reason alone!'

The attorney's expression told her exactly what he was thinking. She should never have allowed herself to be trapped into a position like this, but she had foolishly never given it a thought. She had been too busy falling in love with a man who had nothing but contempt for her. She had never stopped to consider the consequences, and now she would have to harvest what she had sown.

'I'm afraid I can't help you, Kate.' This statement from Hubert Walton came as no surprise to her now. 'This is a problem no one else can solve for you.'

She was on her own. Common sense should have told her it would be this way and, extricating her hand gently from Hubert's, she got to her feet. 'Thanks for listening anyway,' she said absently, and her smile was tight when she kissed him on his leathery cheek and walked out of his office.

She could never quite recall afterwards show she managed to drive herself back to Solitaire without having an accident along the way, and when Edwina questioned her about her visit to the doctor she made some vague reference to dyspepsia which she hoped would satisfy her aunt.

For the next few days Kate behaved like an automaton; doing what she had to do, and speaking only when she was spoken to. Subconsciously, though, she guarded her secret, and when that peculiar numbness finally deserted her she wondered frantically how long it would be before it became obvious to everyone that she was pregnant.

She dreaded the mornings. She took particular care to hide the fact from Rhyno and Aunt Edwina that nausea often drove her from the breakfast table into her bathroom, but for some obscure reason Rhyno followed her one morning. He walked into the bathroom without knocking, and found her puking lustily into the basin.

'For pity's sake, go away and leave me alone!' she cried frantically when she became aware of his tall, lean presence.

'You're ill, Kate,' he observed unnecessarily.

'It must be something I ate.'

'Don't be ridiculous, you hardly ate anything this morning,' he contradicted sharply.

'Please . . .' she begged, leaning weakly against the basin. 'Just go away and let me be sick on my own.'

'Dammit, Kate, I want to help you!'

'I don't need your help, I——' She tried to shrug off his hands, but yet another bout of nausea swept over her, and she was forced to endure his humiliating presence there with her.

'You're not pregnant, are you?' he asked at length when her nausea had abated, and he had helped her wipe her face and rinse her mouth.

'*No!*' she almost screamed at him in her desperation to hide the truth. 'I told you it must be something I ate.'

'You're lying!' he accused harshly, his hands biting into her shoulders as he swung her round to face him.

'I'm not! I'm——' His eyes, searchingly intent on her white face, prevented her from repeating her lie, and she lowered her eyes as she struggled helplessly to escape from those steely fingers. 'Oh, leave me alone, will you?'

'Kate——'

'Damn you, Rhyno, I said leave me alone!' she cried, fear driving her to anger, and she pummelled his chest with her clenched fists in an effort to escape him, but with a muttered oath on his lips he lifted her like a child and carried her into the bedroom.

It was useless trying to fight against the iron-hard strength of those arms imprisoning her. Physically he was her superior, but mentally she would fight him to the bitter end, she decided when he lowered her on to the bed and held her there with the weight of his body.

'I'm not a fool, Kate,' he said, his face dark and threatening above hers. 'I'm well aware of the fact that we've done nothing to prevent you from having a child, and if you're pregnant then I have a right to know.'

'As far as I'm concerned you forfeited all your rights when you forced yourself on me in the first place!'

'Then you are pregnant?' he insisted, his eyes narrowed and intent.

'Yes, damn you, and it's all your fault!' she confessed at last with all the agony of her pent-up fury and despair in her voice.

'Oh, Kate . . .'

'And I shall never forgive you for doing this to me!' she spat out the words. 'The last thing on earth I ever wanted was to have your child!'

'What do you mean by that?'

'Exactly what I said,' she replied, uncaring and too distraught to see the pain in his eyes. 'I don't want your child.'

Rhyno went strangely white. 'You don't know what you're saying.'

'Oh, I know, all right,' she laughed, but her laughter hid the tears that were so horrifyingly close. 'I can't alter the fact that I'm going to have your child, but nothing on earth will force me to stay married to you because of it.'

He eased himself away from her slightly, but he did not release her, and those dark eyes raking her were like a physical punishment. 'You enjoy hurting me, don't you?'

'Do you think I haven't been hurt too? Do you think I enjoy being married to a man who has only contempt for me? Who considers that I possess none of the qualities he could admire in a woman?'

'Look at me, Kate,' he ordered quietly, and when she refused to obey he caught her chin between his fingers and forced her to meet his dark, disturbing eyes as they probed hers relentlessly. 'We've both said hurtful things in the heat of the moment, but . . . I love you, Kate.'

What he had said did not sink in at first, and when it

did it filled her with nothing but bitterness. He was saying that simply because of the child, and resentment and suspicion flowed like poison through her veins as she cried hoarsely, '*No, you don't!*'

'Yes, I do!' he persisted in a rough, unfamiliar voice. 'I've loved you from that first day we met when you looked at me with so much resentment and dislike in your beautiful eyes. I knew then that I had to have you some day, but, God knows, I never wanted it the way your father dreamed it up, with La Reine and Solitaire as bait to urge us into a marriage we weren't ready for.'

'You didn't have to marry me,' she pointed out, deaf to everything except her own misery and pain.

'I could afford to lose La Reine, Kate, but I couldn't let you lose Solitaire.' His expression was grim, and his jaw resolute. 'My mother and I went through that hell once, and I couldn't just sit back and let you suffer.'

Cynicism curved her lovely mouth. 'I suppose I should thank you for that.'

'Is your heart really as hard as flint or stone?' he asked, his words prodding her memory and forcing her to recall those words underlined on those yellowed pages of the book she had found at La Reine. *Hard is her heart as flint or stone, she laughs to see me pale.* He knew that she had seen it. He knew! But she could not believe that it referred to her. 'Are you never going to look at me without resentment and dislike in your eyes?' he asked quietly.

She felt confused and bewildered, and his nearness was not helping her to think coherently either. She wanted to believe him, but she dared not; not until she was sure, and it was with this thought in mind that she said tiredly, 'I don't resent you, and I don't dislike you. As a matter of fact I don't feel anything at the moment except the need to be left alone.'

She thought, at first, that he would not react to her

plea, but a few seconds later she was alone in the room, and she shivered as if he had taken the warmth with him.

She remained there on the bed for a long time, her mind in a frantic turmoil. Rhyno had said that he loved her, that he had loved her from the moment they had met, but had he really meant it, or had he merely said so out of a sense of duty towards her? If only she could be sure!

He did not come home for lunch that day, and neither did he join them for tea in the living-room that afternoon. Kate felt his absence like a lead weight in her chest, and the tears were so close that she constantly had to blink them away, or swallow down the lump in her throat.

'How much longer are you going to keep me in the dark, Kate?' her aunt demanded unexpectedly, her agitated voice intruding into Kate's troubled thoughts. 'Do you think I haven't suspected that something happened between you and Rhyno while I was away, and that you're pregnant?'

'I'm sorry, Aunt Edwina,' Kate gulped, astonished and embarrassed.

'Well?' her aunt demanded. 'Are you pregnant, or aren't you?'

'I am,' Kate admitted, biting down hard on her quivering lip.

'Have you told Rhyno?'

'He knows.'

'And?'

'And nothing,' Kate replied bluntly, desperately pretending not to care. 'Instead of an annulment we shall be divorcing each other, that's all.'

'Kate!'

'Don't look so shocked, Aunt Edwina,' Kate laughed, but her laughter sounded hollow to her own ears. 'Everything will go ahead as planned.'

'What about the child?' her aunt demanded fiercely. 'Do you intend to raise it without the help of its father?'

'I don't particularly want to think about that yet,' Kate replied distastefully.

'You'll have to think about it sooner or later.'

'I suppose so.'

'Kate . . .' Edwina had a way of commanding one's complete attention, and when their eyes met, she asked, 'Are you in love with Rhyno?'

'No!' Kate croaked, averting her eyes.

'Kate? You can tell me the truth, my dear. Are you in love with him?'

Kate's resistance crumbled as always at the note of tenderness in her aunt's voice and, with a little choked cry, she buried her face in her hands and whispered brokenly through her tears, 'Oh, Aunt Edwina . . . I've never been so—so unhappy in all my—my life!'

Tears never really solved anything, her aunt reminded her when she finally managed to control herself, and when Rhyno also refrained from joining them for dinner that evening, Aunt Edwina said: 'I suggest the two of you thrash out this problem when he comes home this evening.'

Kate finally agreed, but she had no idea just how to go about it. What would she say to him? And how would she know if he were telling her the truth?

She was in bed when Rhyno came in late that night and, shivering with nerves, she pulled the blankets closer about her. 'What am I going to say?' she wondered again. 'How do I begin this probe for the truth?'

She heard him moving about in the dressing-room, but indecision held her captive until she heard the catches of a suitcase being snapped shut. The sound vaulted her out of bed and, pulling on her robe, she ran barefoot across the carpeted floor and wrenched open the door.

'What are you doing?' she demanded, her voice a mere croak and her face white and pinched when she saw Rhyno flinging his clothes into the suitcase that stood open on his bed.

'I'm moving back to La Reine, and no one need know that except us.'

'But why?'

He glanced at her only briefly, but long enough for her to recoil inwardly from the cold, hard stab of his eyes. 'Isn't it obvious?'

'I'm afraid not,' she confessed in an agonised whisper.

'You said this morning that you wanted to be left alone, and the only way I can do that is to move back to La Reine.'

'But—but I——' Her voice faltered and she swallowed convulsively. He could think her shameless, he could think what he wished, but she knew now that she could not let him go; not like this, and not without shedding the remnants of her pride in letting him know how she felt about him. 'You—you told me this morning that—that you loved me,' she managed at length.

'Did I?'

'You know you did.'

'I must have been out of my mind!' he snarled, thrusting a pair of socks into the corner of the suitcase and slamming down the lid.

'You didn't mean it?' she questioned unsteadily, biting down hard on her quivering lip, and going a shade paler at the naked fury in his eyes when he swung round to face her.

'If you expect me to grovel at your feet, Kate, then you can forget it. I'm moving back to La Reine, and I'll stay there until our distasteful marriage is at an end.'

They stood facing each other in silence, the tension spiralling between them until it was almost tangible, and

Kate no longer felt so sure of herself. A few months ago she would have had no difficulty in finding something to say, but at that moment she could think of nothing which would prevent Rhyno from leaving Solitaire. She knew, irrevocably, that if she let him go he would need to take only one more step to walk right out of her life, and her aching heart warned that she dared not let that happen. It no longer mattered whether he had meant it that morning when he had said that he loved her. She loved him enough to make their marriage work, if only he would give her the opportunity to try.

'Rhyno . . .' His name was a mere breath on her quivering lips, and she held out her hands in an appealing gesture. 'Don't go . . . please don't go.'

He ignored her hands, and she clasped them nervously and a little self-consciously in front of her as if she didn't quite know what to do with them. His eyes were stabbingly intent, probing hers as if to sear her very soul, but she did not look away even though she kept the shutters down defensively from force of habit. She dared not let him see too much for fear of being rejected. She could, at least save herself that final humiliation.

'Give me one good reason why I should stay?' he demanded coldly.

Her nerve ends quivered uncomfortably, and her mouth went dry. She knew of only one good reason why he should stay, but she shrank inwardly from voicing it. He was watching her intently, his face an unrelenting mask, and something warned her that this was not the moment to cling to her worthless pride. She ran her tongue across her lips and, taking a careful breath, risked her soul on the table of chance.

'I didn't mean it this morning when I said I didn't want your child. I do want it, but I was afraid, and I went a little crazy, I think.' His expression remained un-

altered, and she felt herself shaking. 'I love you,' the words
were finally torn from her heart in a husky voice.

'Do you?' he smiled cynically, and it sliced her to the
core.

'Oh, God!' she groaned, weak with despair as she
leaned shakily against the wall and pressed her hands flat
against its hard coolness.

'How do I know you're not saying that because you've
suddenly realised the difficulties in bringing up a child on
your own?' he demanded harshly, and in that moment of
sanity she realised that he was taunting her, and hurting
her in much the same way she had done to him that
morning.

'Expecting your child makes no difference to the way I
feel,' she argued quietly.

'Then prove it.'

Her heart thumped against her ribs. 'How?'

'That's the problem,' he replied at once, with such bitterness and cynicism in his voice that she winced inwardly.
'How do we prove that what we feel for each other is not
simply because of the child? Or because of La Reine and
Solitaire?'

'Rhyno . . .?' she questioned breathlessly, her heart
suddenly beating so fast that it seemed to choke her as she
looked up into eyes that seemed to be burning down into
hers with such an intensity of feeling it made her feel
strangely dizzy.

'We'll have to trust each other,' he was saying, standing
so close to her now that she could feel the disturbing heat
of his body against her own, then he framed her face
gently with his hands. 'Do you trust me, Kate?'

She began to tremble with an exquisite, aching joy,
and tears of happiness brimmed her eyes, distorting her
vision of the tender smile she had waited so long to see.

'I've been such a fool,' she whispered brokenly, burying

her face against him, and her answer seemed to satisfy him, for he drew her closer to the hard, comforting length of him.

'We've both been fools in one way or another.'

'Will you forgive me?' she pleaded, loving the feel of his fingers moving through her hair.

'I have nothing to forgive.'

'I've said some terrible things in the past, and I've accused you unjustly on so many occasions that I——'

His lips bruised hers into silence with a searing kiss that left her limp and yielding in his arms. She slipped her arms about his waist, pressing closer to him as their kiss deepened with a new hunger as they drank the sweet nectar of so late a harvest. His hands caressed her, moulding her into the hard curve of his body, and she fumbled with his shirt buttons to bring herself closer still to his warm flesh.

'I love you, Kate. Don't ever doubt that,' he groaned against her soft, eager mouth, then he lifted her in his arms and carried her into the bedroom.

There was still so much to talk about, but it could wait, Kate decided as the flame of passion leapt between them. They made love fiercely, tenderly, holding nothing back, and free at last to give all on the altar of their love.

Later, when they lay quietly in each others arms, Kate could not help murmuring, 'My father was perhaps wiser than both of us.'

'I'm not in the mood to argue with that,' Rhyno replied, and the sound of his soft, throaty laughter thrilled her almost as much as the hand that came up to clasp her breast. There was a renewed hunger in the mouth that found hers without difficulty in the moonlit darkness of the room, and her need rose swiftly once more to meet his.

*

Six months later, on the anniversary of their wedding, Hubert Walton arrived at Solitaire to carry out Jacques Duval's final instructions. His glance travelled only briefly over Edwina, Naomi, and Rhyno, then it settled on Kate, and he smiled affectionately as he took in her full figure beneath the wide maternity dress.

'Don't keep us in suspense, Uncle Hubert,' she said with only the briefest touch of anxiety in her voice. 'You know very well that we're going to continue with our marriage, so what new twist in my father's will has necessitated this meeting?'

Hubert laughed a little drily and produced an envelope from his briefcase. 'Your father wrote two letters before he died, and it depended on your decision which one was to be opened on this day.'

Kate glanced at Rhyno on the sofa beside her, and her hand sought and found his before she faced the attorney and said: 'You'd better open the letter and read it to us.'

The grey-haired man nodded and slid his thumb beneath the flap of the envelope. Kate recognised her father's bold handwriting even from a distance, and her fingers tightened almost convulsively about Rhyno's when Hubert cleared his throat and read its contents out aloud.

'My dear children,' the letter began, 'Of the two letters I hope that this is the one being read to you, as it has always been my wish to not only unite La Reine and Solitaire, but to unite my daughter with the son of the woman I had loved so dearly in my youth.

'This is not, however, the time to become maudlin. I congratulate you on the anniversary of your wedding day, and I would like to express the wish that you may share long and happy years together.

'There is one matter I wish to clear up. Rhyno, when your father left your mother destitute, and after the eventual news of his death, I asked Naomi to marry me, but she had some unshakable notion that it would be unfair to accept my proposal. When the situation at La Reine became desperate I knew that she would be too proud to accept financial help from me, so I did the next best thing. I bought La Reine to preserve it for you, and I financed your studies secretly to prepare you for the day when I hoped you would take over its management.'

'*Damn!*' Rhyno exploded, interrupting the reading of Jacques' letter as he leapt to his feet to face Naomi. 'Did you know this, Mother?' he demanded angrily.

'I guessed . . . but I was never sure.'

'And you let him do it?' Rhyno thundered incredulously.

'You know Jacques,' Naomi smiled warily at her son. 'Was he the kind of man one could go to and say, "Are you financing my son's education, and if you are would you please stop it"?'

Rhyno continued to glare at no one in particular, and a new fear shifted stealthily into Kate's heart. Her husband was a proud man, and this disclosure was not something he would come to terms with very easily.

'Shall I continue?' Hubert interrupted the tense silence.

'You mean there's more?' Rhyno barked, swinging round to face the attorney, and Hubert nodded as he unfolded the letter and continued reading.

'Knowing you, Rhyno, I don't doubt that you're furious. Your pride has been dented, but look at it from my point of view. Feeling about your mother the way I did, I always looked upon you as my son and, had she married me, I would have had every right to finance your studies openly. I followed your progress closely, and your mother, unknowingly, helped me to decide when the time would be right to tempt you with an offer which would bring you back to La Reine.

'You always said that I was a shrewd old man, and you were right. I knew that I had little time left, and delivering that ultimatum in my will was the only way I could think of inducing you to accept La Reine. I guessed how you felt about Kate, and I hoped that the possibility of her losing Solitaire might be enough instigation for you to marry her, thus securing your own, as well as her inheritance.

'Forgive me, Kate, for using you as the instrument to carry out my plans, but I did so with the sure knowledge that you would be safe with Rhyno. There is nothing else to say except to ask you both not to judge me too harshly.'

The silence that followed was strained and tense with emotions that hovered awkwardly between understanding and displeasure, but Edwina, who had remained silent throughout the reading of Jacques' letter, stepped swiftly into the breach with the ever practical suggestion.

'I think we could all do with a nice cup of tea,' she announced briskly, but Hubert shook his head.

'Not for me, Edwina,' he said. 'I must go back to the office.' He rose as he spoke and turned to Rhyno. 'We can settle the last of the legal matters tomorrow if you and Kate could come to my office some time during the morning.'

Rhyno nodded, but he was looking at Kate, and what she saw in his eyes chilled her considerably. He had not taken her father's disclosures lightly, and although she did not doubt his love for her, she feared that it might affect their future happiness.

It was not until that evening, when they were alone in their bedroom that they had the opportunity to speak privately to each other.

'It's not very pleasant knowing that your father is responsible for everything I am today,' he confessed grimly when he emerged from his shower and seated himself on the bed beside Kate. 'How does one repay such a debt?'

'Darling,' she said softly, sitting up in bed to frame his lean, clean-shaven face with her small hands, 'in the past two and a half years you've given so much of yourself to La Reine as well as Solitaire, and what you've given surpasses in value anything and everything my father may have done for you.' She had spoken with a quiet sincerity, but her eyes suddenly sparkled with mischief. 'Added to that you've taken on the lifelong task of taking charge of his impossible, often shrewish daughter, and that, I think, ought to amount to something.'

He took her hands in his and pressed his warm mouth in a sensual caress against each palm. 'Taking charge of you has been a pleasure, not a duty.'

'Has it always been a pleasure?' she asked with a smile that was impish even though it radiated an unmistakable warmth. 'Even when I accused you of ingratiating yourself with my father, and heaven only knows what else?'

'You resented the conditions in your father's will as much as I did, and that was your way of kicking against it.'

'How did you deal with your resentment?'

His eyes mocked her tenderly. 'Dealing with you fortunately took up most of my time and energy.'

'I'm not sure I like the sound of that,' she laughed lightly, 'but I'll let it pass.'

'You're obviously in a generous mood.'

Her expression sobered with sincerity. 'I happen to love you very much, that's all.'

'That's everything,' Rhyno corrected, drawing her into his arms and kissing her with a tenderness that never failed to touch her deeply. 'You are all that I could ever have wished for, and this . . .' he placed his hand very gently on her rounded stomach, 'this is an added bonus.'

Their lips met and clung, and in a rush of tender passion, Kate drew him down beside her, vowing in her heart that she would always endeavour to be worthy of this proud man's love—until the late harvest of their lives and beyond.

Harlequin® Plus
A WORD ABOUT THE AUTHOR

Yvonne Whittal's childhood was spent in Port Elizabeth, on the southern tip of Africa. She recalls dreaming of the day she would be able to travel to unknown countries.

At a very early age she began scribbling stories. Her ambition to be a writer resurfaced after her marriage and the birth of three daughters. She enrolled in a writing course, began submitting short stories to publishers and, with each rejection letter, became all the more determined.

Turning to the task of writing a full-length book, Yvonne was encouraged by a young woman with whom she was working—an avid reader of romance fiction and a helpful critic.

For Yvonne Whittal, there is no greater satisfaction than writing. "The characters become part of my life," she says, "and when I come to the end of each novel, realizing that I now have to part with my manuscript, it is like saying farewell to dear and trusted friends."

Legacy of
PASSION
BY CATHERINE KAY

A love story begun long ago comes full circle…

Venice, 1819: Contessa Allegra di Rienzi, young, innocent, unhappily married. She gave her love to Lord Byron—scandalous, irresistible English poet. Their brief, tempestuous affair left her with a shattered heart, a few poignant mementos—and a daughter he never knew about.

Boston, today: Allegra Brent, modern, independent, restless. She learned the secret of her great-great-great-grandmother and journeyed to Venice to find the di Rienzi heirs. There she met the handsome, cynical, blood-stirring Conte Renaldo di Rienzi, and like her ancestor before her, recklessly, hopelessly lost her heart.

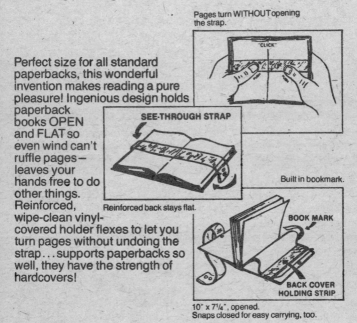

Readers rave about Harlequin romance fiction...

"I absolutely adore Harlequin romances! They are fun and relaxing to read, and each book provides a wonderful escape."
—N.E.,* Pacific Palisades, California

"Harlequin is the best in romantic reading."
—K.G., Philadelphia, Pennsylvania

"Harlequin romances give me a whole new outlook on life."
—S.P., Mecosta, Michigan

"My praise for the warmth and adventure your books bring into my life."
—D.F., Hicksville, New York

*Names available on request.

SUPERROMANCE

Longer, exciting, sensuous and dramatic!

Fascinating love stories that will hold
you in their magical spell till the last page
is turned!

Now's your chance to discover the earlier
books in this exciting series. Choose from
the great selection on the following page!

Choose from this list of great
SUPERROMANCES!

SUPERROMANCE

Complete and mail this coupon today!
